Down in the Valley

ALSO BY PAOLO COGNETTI

The Eight Mountains
Without Ever Reaching the Summit
The Lovers

Down in the Valley

PAOLO COGNETTI

Translated from the Italian
by Stash Luczkiw

Harvill
Secker

1 3 5 7 9 10 8 6 4 2

Harvill Secker, an imprint of Vintage, is part of the Penguin
Random House group of companies

Vintage, Penguin Random House UK, One Embassy Gardens,
8 Viaduct Gardens, London SW11 7BW

penguin.co.uk/vintage
global.penguinrandomhouse.com

Penguin
Random House
UK

First published by Harvill Secker in 2025

Typeset in 13.3/18.2pt Calluna by Jouve (uk), Milton Keynes
Printed and bound in Great Britain by Clays Ltd, Elcograf S.p.A.

The authorised representative in the EEA is Penguin Random House Ireland,
Morrison Chambers, 32 Nassau Street, Dublin D02 YH68

A CIP catalogue record for this book is available from the British Library

ISBN 9781787304994

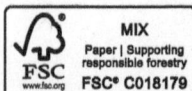

The Grant

It's either this or bobcat hunting
with my friend Morris.
Trying to write a poem at six this
morning, or else running
behind the hounds with
a rifle in my hands.
Heart jumping in its cage.
I'm 45 years old. No occupation.
Imagine the luxuriousness of this life.
Try and imagine.
May go with him if he goes
tomorrow. But may not.

Raymond Carver

Valsesia

She was a female who had not yet seen her second winter, nor any world other than the car repair shop along the country road. Alone, in the back of the garage, she was playing with the shred of an old tyre: she bit it, tossed it, ran to catch it, then realised she had spectators. A grey dog had appeared from the gravel pit nearby and was watching her. There was the river on that side, even though it was shallow in the autumn, and didn't take much to ford. She set the piece of rubber down to sniff the air for that male's scent, but as she raised her snout, she saw three more poking out from the scrap heap. Three shepherds with muddy fur and bells in their collars, but these she knew. During the day, they looked after the sheep, grazing on the stubble in the fields and the grass around the sheds, and in the evening they wandered around looking for something to steal. But now they weren't there for the food – they were there for her. The female both knew and didn't know why they had come. She was just over a year old, and this new male interest in her was among the things she was learning quickly, things as exciting and dangerous as the bonfires boys lit in the summer, or the river's current, which had once almost taken her away.

There was a car seat uprooted, set against the workshop wall, where she went to crouch. A car seat that had hosted generations of dogs before her. Not far away, the backhoe sank its arm into the riverbed, pulled up a bucket of sand and gravel, and at that moment the grey dog made a move to get closer. The three shepherds re-established their hierarchies: a growl and a glimpse of his teeth were enough for the older and larger one to make the second stand down and whimper as he withdrew; the third was already walking away. Then the leader advanced with small steps, according to a male ritual that the female knew. Threatening, growling, baring his teeth – this was how the dogs of the valley fought – but the grey one came from another place where he had been brought up differently, by men or by life. When the leader raised his hackles, stiffening to impress him, the grey dog sprang at him without any preamble. He was the skinnier of the two, but the impact was enough to tip the other onto his back, then he blocked him with a paw and sank his teeth into his throat. The female had never seen this done. She felt a new thrill as the grey dog tightened his grip, refusing to let go of the struggling shepherd's throat. Until even his friends, who were pacing around restlessly, saw their leader's body go limp, his neck spewing blood and the blood soaking the dirt road. Now even he looked like an old tyre, and after a moment the other two disappeared into the fields.

A tanker passed by on the country road. It had a smattering of frost on its roof, which flew away with a puff. November. The female got off her car seat and wagged her tail at the male as he approached. The fury of only moments ago had already subsided in him. She smelled him gently, she let herself be smelled. The scent she picked up was of the forest, of earth, leaves, and the blood of the dog he had just killed. She felt like licking it, and she licked it. Then he took her and just like that her infancy was finished forever.

*

They went upriver that day, running all giddy for having met each other, along gravel banks and islets, across the wastelands of the valley floor. The distant ridges were marked by snow, but along the river there were cement factories, furniture factories, agro-wholesalers and construction warehouses. They saw mice in the ditches and crows in the landfills, they smelled the fertiliser spread in the fields, and when they found human beings – in a van on the bank – she, who had no fear of humans, understood that he avoided them, because they waded back into the river again to continue on the other bank. They skirted a fence, and their trail ended at a lock where the river was blocked and the conduits started. From there, they could hear traffic on the road, somewhere beyond the levee. The light was fading, and he wanted to wait for darkness before coming out into the open. As they waited she became hungry. She hadn't put anything into her stomach for hours, and she made him understand the way puppies do, licking and nibbling his snout, as if he were her father and had to get her food. Deep down he appreciated that torment.

In the dark, he led her along the road to a building that had a large neon sign on the front, a ball that intermittently rolled towards some pins. Behind it, a metal door and a small opaque window gave out onto the parking lot, and a dog tied outside heard them coming. It was a little one, barking and pulling on his lead while they remained hidden where the light didn't reach. After a minute the little dog stopped, stared into the darkness, heard another one barking somewhere else and answered back, then the metal door opened and a boy in a white apron came out. The little dog wagged its tail all happy. The boy threw two trash bags against the wall, looked at the starless and moonless sky and took something from his pocket, which he handed to the dog, stroking its head as it ate from his hand.

That sight stirred in the female, hidden between the cars, a feeling she had never felt before – a sort of nostalgia. It was the petting, not the food. The boy's affection and the dog's unconditional trust. The male didn't give her any more time. He came out of the darkness as soon as the boy went back to the kitchen. The little dog raised its nose from the bowl, but it was useless and couldn't do much tied up like that. A maw caught its throat before it could even bark. It let out a gasp and a hiss.

No one from the kitchen heard and no one came to see, and by the time the female reached them it was already dead: sprawled with its mouth open, tongue sticking out. Her lover was not interested in the dog and moved towards the trash bags, tearing at them with his nails and teeth. They found a bounty of meat, pasta and bones, and ate their fill next to that corpse tied to its lead while the neon ball knocked the pins down under the dark sky.

*

In the villages throughout the Valsesia, where winter was descending on the right and left banks of the river, rumours began to spread about these dead dogs – the shepherd, then the bowling-alley mutt, then a hunting dog that had gone into the woods and never returned, then the guard dog at a sawmill – and of their killer, who dispatched them all in the same way, all male. In the bars, where the news spread, there were those who bet that it was a wolf. Only wolves killed like that – or did they? Others thought he was a game-bred fighting dog escaped from his owner, who was careful not to report him. Then the theory took shape that it was half-and-half, one of those cross-breeds between

8

stray dogs and wolves, like mutations you would hear about. Diabolical beings because they had two souls: a dog's familiarity with man, and the ferocity of the wolf. In local legends, they approached meekly and then suddenly attacked. But the theory created a problem, because a rabid dog could and indeed should be killed, but not a wolf, which was protected by law. So what to do with a hybrid? Discussions livened up the bar at happy hour. Over a second glass of Bonarda, or a Campari with white wine, another round of the same as before, it was said, not even so quietly, that the forestry police were sitting on their hands. They preferred giving fines to protecting the citizens. Okay, so far, there was no word of attacks on humans, but what mother in those days would have left a child outside to play? In any case, it was hunting season, and there were many hunters in the valley. Hunting for wild boar, chamois, deer, blondes . . . The men had fun like this. They would insinuate and nudge each other, chuck a couple of peanuts into their mouths and wink at the waitress. Then they would drain the dregs of their glasses, pay for the round, get into their pick-up trucks and go back home to their wives for dinner. If any dog-shaped beast crossed their path, they would gun it down without a second thought.

*

That night she dreamed of her mother. She dreamed she was so young that she still lived attached to her mother, together with her brothers and sisters. Outside of her dream she moved her paws, moaned softly, and in her dream she competed for a teat with the other puppies like herself. There were men around, not actual faces but presences, voices, and then a hand dropped from those voices. It was bigger than her, she felt the bulk of it on her, the fingers around her body, the hand that took her and pulled her up.

She woke up from the fright and found herself in the dark without knowing where she was. First, she recognised the scent of her lover, his thick fur and skin-and-bone ribcage. That smell of his had the power to calm her down immediately. Then, slowly, she sensed all the rest in the night surrounding them: the concrete pillar of the bridge where they had found shelter, a car passing above them, the river's gurgling. She didn't know how many days they had been climbing it. Nor did she wonder where the male was taking her – she just followed him. He watched over her, even now: the rhythm of his breath telling her he was resting, but not asleep.

Early in the morning, as they continued through the woods, she saw movement in the middle of the river. She sniffed the air and caught the scent of a woman. She knew how to distinguish it from that of a man. She was intrigued by it. She let the male go ahead and ventured to the edge of the vegetation, near the water.

The woman was walking into a pool. She had very white skin and red hair. It was cold. Her breath steamed, yet she entered the river one step at a time. The water had reached her thighs when she felt she was being watched, so she turned towards the bushes and saw her. Their gazes met. The little dog felt that feeling again, that nostalgia.

Her lover was beside her now. He also watched the woman, and the woman watched them both. Then her male nudged her neck with his muzzle and went on his way. She was afraid that if she stayed, he would leave her, so she left the woman in the water, gave in and followed him.

*

Later, the landscape changed and the mixed woodland on the valley floor gave way to conifers and sparser birches. Slender birches lined the banks, with dense woods behind them. Even the river – which downstream was always blocked, dammed, dried up by water intakes – flowed freely here among the stones, and where one of its bends turned north, they suddenly found snow. Only a veil of snow that had fallen a few days ago, preserved in the shade. The dog smelled it and recognised the scent that had come to her from far away on other occasions. She wanted to taste it and discovered that the snow was not food, but a game. She scratched that frozen crust with her nails, buried her muzzle in it, sneezed, filled her mouth and ears with it again.

Meanwhile, the male had found a shack made of wood and sheet metal. A chimney came out of the roof but without any smoke. He sniffed around, found no danger, followed a scent that led him to a grill placed on two bricks. There was some meat fat congealed on the grill. More fat had fallen into the ash and he began digging for something he had smelled.

It was she who saw the dog leap out of the woods, running, big and black. He ran at the grey one and bit his right side. Taken by surprise, the grey one managed to turn around and bite where he could, but the teeth were planted in his flesh and wouldn't let go. She saw them rolling between the river water and snow. She whimpered in anguish, not knowing how to intervene. Several times the two males pinned and overturned each other, until, fighting blindly, the grey dog had a stroke of luck. The black one wound up with his neck bent under the weight of both of them, and she heard the sound of it cracking. His jaws opened immediately. The black dog stayed on the ground shaking – he couldn't get back to his feet – and the grey one, with all the rage he had in his body, was at his throat. He put so much force into it that he tore off his leather collar.

He was victim number eight of their spree. They left quickly and later she helped take care of him. He had a nasty gash on his flank, right where his ribs ended along the soft flesh of his abdomen. She licked him, his blood tasted no different from that of the dogs he had killed. She licked his wound, cleaned the dirt from it, licked into his raw flesh, but couldn't make it stop bleeding.

*

The ninth was just a stray who had ended up among the rubbish bins at the wrong time, and the tenth was one who had followed the female's scent and would have been better off staying in his yard. Ten innocent dogs, ten males killed in a few days.

The last night they spent under a rock that protruded enough to hide and shelter them. She wasn't sleeping any more either, now. She listened to him panting and licking his wound and shifting position, and at a certain point high up, in the strip of black sky above them, the moon appeared. An autumn moon that reached the riverbed, the snow on its banks, and made it glimmer faintly: snow gathering light sent by the moon. The male, surprised by that glow, raised his head and pricked up his ears. He stared at the moon, sniffed, listened as if he was waiting for a voice, something or someone to call him, but in the night there was nothing but the incessant flow of the river.

At dawn, they were still together between two steep banks and large stranded trunks brought down by the floods. He led the way in front of her, limping and bleeding, though still seeming to know his destination, when she saw the dogs coming. They were hunting dogs, chasing the smell of blood and barking when they sensed their prey. They went right by, ignoring her. The male started running with what little strength he had. The hounds chased him, pushed him to change direction. As soon as he stepped out into the open, a shot cracked high up, somewhere above the river. His legs suddenly gave way. He fell and rolled down into the water, into the current.

The female crouched, terrified. The echo of the shot died out and she raised her eyes to look up at the slope. She heard a whistle, and the hounds took off towards their master, disappearing as quickly as they had come. She didn't move: she was a clear target, which seemed to offer itself to their aim. But the second shot never came.

When she was able to move again, she went down to the river and approached the male lying among the rocks. She nuzzled him, sniffed his neck and chest. She found the bullet hole, the blood flowing away with the water. She sniffed his ears, his mouth, that good, familiar smell that was already fading. She had seen ten dogs dead in a few days, and a week before she had been no more than a puppy. Now she recognised death and knew that her lover was gone, that the body there in the river was just flesh and bone, like the others. She looked around, still undecided about the direction, then walked away with her ears down in the direction of the current, from where they had come.

Forestry Cop

From their bed, in the afternoon, they could see the sign of the petrol station, an artificial moon that lit up over the valley as soon as darkness fell. Elisabetta was lying on her side. She looked at the branches of the trees against that electric yellow, and Luigi caressed her from behind. The line of her shoulder, her collarbone, her breast. Her breasts were changing. She was getting fuller as the weeks went by, and it seemed to him that her nipples were getting thicker. He caressed one with his fingers under the covers.

He said: Do you think she can hear us when we fight?

Of course she can hear us, Elisabetta said.

What does she hear?

She hears and feels through me. She can sense that I'm not well.

And when we make love?

Sure. That too.

So she's happy when we make love?

No, she's jealous.

Jealous of her father!

Luigi traced the ribs to her belly, which was just beginning to grow. The scar above her navel, the soft down. He felt like he knew that body even better than his own.

He said: Aren't all little girls in love with their father?

That happens later. If . . .

If?

If he's a good father.

I get it.

It's dark already. What time is it?

It's time to go.

Begrudgingly, Luigi detached himself from his wife's body and turned to the other side of the bed. He checked his watch: a quarter to three. He pulled back the covers, sat down, retrieved his underwear and socks from where they had ended up. He stood naked in the yellow light, his torso pale and his neck dark from the sun.

He went into the bathroom, turned the tap

on the sink. He took a sip of water and tasted the chlorine they threw in to disinfect it. This was something he had never got used to. When he came back, Elisabetta, with her underwear on, had changed position. She was sitting up against her pillow, her red hair falling across her shoulders. He opened his uniform wardrobe.

She said: You wanna go out in this cold?

Eh, like it or not.

Should I wait for you for dinner?

I don't think so. I'm seeing my brother later.

He put on his grey-green shirt and trousers, slipped into his jacket, took the big belt and tightened it to the usual hole. It was black, with the holster on the right side. The insignia on the breast pocket of his jacket read: STATE FORESTRY CORPS.

Look, she said. Why don't you take him to a hotel? We'll pay for it. What can it cost in the low season?

My brother, in a hotel?

I'm sorry. I don't want your brother in the house.

I know, I know.

Agent Luigi Balma leaned over to say goodbye to his wife. Now it was she who caressed him. She wanted to hold him a little longer. She straightened his collar and brushed the dust off one shoulder.

Are you coming back late?

No.

Will you promise me you won't drink too much?

How can I promise? I'll try.

He kissed her. Her kiss was longer, his was shorter. Then his shadow passed quickly across the sheets.

*

At the command post, he took the Defender, adjusted the seat to his height, lowered the window and let the cold air in. There was no one with him that day, but Luigi liked going out alone: he didn't have to listen to any chatter and he could smoke. He lit a cigarette and slipped into the road. It was a Wednesday like any other, with hardly any cars in the villages he passed, more bars than folks around, elbows on the counter already at four in the after-noon. The Sesia, when he crossed it, was a dark furrow.

After the bridge, the sides of the valley got steeper. Autumn, by now, had lost all its colour and the dry leaves of the beech, chestnut and oak groves were accumulating on the ground. He raised his eyes from those skeletal woods to the red crests above the three-thousand-metre peaks. A beautiful sunset, even if no one would notice from below. Because of the thermal inversion, smoke from the chimneys would float amid the barns down in the valley. The humidity made the asphalt slick and fogged up the windscreen, whereas up there the stones would warm up in the sun.

He turned left onto a dirt road that led back towards the river. Two hundred metres of mud and puddles. Once past the entrance gate, he heard the screech of a bandsaw and stopped in a courtyard where stacks of boards were seasoning under the sheet-metal canopies. He got out of the four-by-four and waited for someone to show up. Wandering among the stacks, he was drawn to a scent: he found the wood giving it off and stroked it. The resin was still fresh.

About time, someone said.

Luigi turned around. A man of about fifty in overalls. He approached with the heavy steps of a henhouse owner.

I called a while ago, he said.

And here I am, Luigi said.

Alone?

You know how it is, hunting season.

The guy looked at the rank stripe on his pocket. Maybe he knew how to read them, maybe not. They sent the last man in the pecking order.

Nice stone pine, Luigi said. Where's it from?

Austria. All this stuff is Austrian.

It grew up high, though. Tight rings.

I wouldn't know.

Up high in the sun.

You want to see the papers?

No, no. Let me see the dog.

The man led him through the shed, where the machines had not stopped turning. The pine resin stayed on his fingers, and he sniffed it as he walked over a carpet of chips. Two workers watched him pass by: gloves, caps and safety glasses – as if prepared for a visit from a labour inspector. If that's for me, he thought, you could've spared yourself the masquerade.

They went out back and there, among the scraps of wood, was a dog lying on the ground, in a dark stain. Belgian shepherd, at first glance. Black-and-brown male. That shadow all around was the blood that had come out of his throat.

When did you find him? Luigi asked.

This morning, when I opened up.

You leave him here at night?

You bet, to guard the place. That's what a guard dog's for.

What do they steal from here?

Everything. Even the wood.

Did they steal anything last night?

No. Don't seem so.

Luigi bent down and extended a hand towards the dog's muzzle. He was young, with beautiful white teeth. An old leather collar, belonging to others before him. His throat caked with clotted blood. He reached into the thick fur to feel the wound.

They slit his throat, didn't they? the guy said.

Could be.

I know who did it.

No, that wasn't the cut of a knife. It was the gash of teeth fiercer than his. Luigi felt the dog's shoulders and chest for more bites, but he found none. There had been no real fight. On the other hand, he found two broken ribs, the bump where they had joined together badly. And a tick under the armpit as big as a finger. He looked around and noticed the chain, the dirty plastic trays, the dung in the sawdust.

Guard dog, eh? You trained him yourself?

You bet.

With kicks and a cudgel?

He sized the man up and down, looked into his eyes for the first and only time: small, yellow, hostile, and that was all there was to see. He stood up, checked his hand. The dog's blood had stained it slightly.

Is the river back there? he asked.

A fence closed off the courtyard, twisted metal mesh. Beyond the fence, a thicket invaded by brambles and vines.

You guessed it, the guy said.

Luigi wiped his hand on a rag and did the paperwork on the bandsaw table. No matter what he'd been convinced of, the man eventually signed a complaint against unknown culprits. Then one of the workers helped Luigi wrap the dog in a tarp and load it into the Defender.

*

He met his brother that evening in a bar in Borgosesia, near the bus station. They hadn't seen

26

each other for seven years: he found him leaner, his hair longer, a handlebar moustache, but underneath the moustache he was still good-looking, always had been. The same cutting smile stained slightly by smoke. Luigi had stopped noticing his own uniform.

Look at you! Alfredo said.

Look at what?

I've got a cop for a brother.

Ciao, Fredo.

C'mere. Don't play tough guy, c'mon.

His brother put his arm around him. Luigi remained as stiff as a stockfish. The last time, Alfredo had just finished serving an eighteen-month sentence and for a change of scenery went to Canada, where they were looking for people to work in the woods. Yes, now he definitely looked like a Canadian lumberjack. He was the last piece of family Luigi had left.

Oh no, the Balma brothers in action, the bartender said. Should I call the long arm of the law?

The long arm of the law is right here, Alfredo said.

What can I get you?

Tell me, you feel like a local specialty?

Why not, Luigi said.

Two beers and two Canadian Clubs, if you got any.

I've got Canadian Club. You want ice?

No, no. I've seen enough ice.

So now Alfredo was drinking whisky and beer: back in the day he would drink a bottle of bitters in one evening. He was already slurring, and Luigi suspected that he had got a head start in the afternoon. For him, who hadn't had dinner, the first drop of whisky went straight to his head. His throat burned and that's what the beer was for, to douse the burn and go back to the Canadian Club.

Alfredo started talking about his work on the other side of the world. Recently, he had stopped cutting logs and started trucking them, a career move. All the way down to Vancouver, now that's a city, he said. He talked about the coast and meant the Pacific Coast. He travelled from the woods of the Rocky Mountains to the industrial ports where the logs were loaded onto ships, mostly to China.

China? Luigi said.

They buy everything.

Don't they have trees in China?

What do I know? You should see the ships.

Luigi was someone who tended to think that no one really changed in life, but seven years was a long time. Maybe you could change, just a little, in seven years so far from home? He took a sip of whisky and one of beer, picking up the pace while Alfredo described the machines they used to cut down whole mountain slopes. Instead of chainsaws, they mowed the woods down like wheat fields. And those roads in British Columbia with a gas station every hundred kilometres and nothing but lakes and rivers in between. But look at him there, Luigi said to himself: at twelve he was grazing goats in Fontana Fredda, at twenty-seven he was in prison for assault and battery, and at thirty-five he's driving trucks up and down the Canadian coast. He wore his good mood at that bar down in the valley in November like a Hawaiian shirt. He realised he felt affection for him, even without trusting that he had changed.

And you? Alfredo said. You never started working with wood?

I tried.

And then?

And then . . . between the mortgage and the taxes, it was like getting robbed.

So you went over to the thieves.

C'mon, shut up.

I was kidding.

Not because I like it. But a pay cheque's a beautiful thing.

And how. What's that weapon on you?

A Beretta 92.

I got one too, you know, back in the truck. A Glock. For the bears.

Don't tell me.

Are things cool with your wife?

Yeah, they're all right.

There you go.

People walked into the bar; Luigi noticed that they were looking at them. He saw what they saw: a forestry cop in uniform and some dude with long hair; four empty glasses on the counter. While the bartender served the second round, he told Alfredo he was going to the car to get cigarettes.

There was a telephone booth across the street. He went in, looked for a coin and dialled home. Elisabetta didn't answer. For a minute, Luigi listened to the phone ringing. He knew why she wouldn't answer. Now he had to find a bed for his brother. But it was early. It wasn't even nine.

He went into the truck, not the service Defender, but his old Suzuki. He took off his jacket and belt, put on the hunting jacket he kept in the back. He hid the gun in the glove compartment. Before getting out of the car, he looked at himself in the mirror, rubbing his eyes in the harsh dome light inside. Will you promise me you won't drink too much? she had said. She had taken his hand and brought it to her breast. He imagined the phone ringing and her sitting in the kitchen, letting it ring.

He went back to the bar. Alfredo was talking with the two men who had just walked in. Alarm bells went off for Luigi: his brother alone at the counter and the two at the table. Then he realised that they were the ones in a heated discussion. Fredo was just watching. Faces he knew but couldn't connect to names.

One said: Ask him if it ain't true!

And the other: Get outta here.

Luigi headed for his cold beer, foam overflowing. Alfredo seemed amused by the conversation. He saved them the trouble and said: What's this about some wolf going around killing dogs?

Who said it's a wolf? Luigi asked.

Half-dog, half-wolf, one of the two said.

That's just bar talk.

So what is it, then?

A puma.

Alfredo laughed. Luigi moved the stool and sat between him and them. An old reflex.

Okay, boss, if you feel like messing with us . . .

Must be a game-bred dog, no?

A fighting dog? the other guy said.

That's what you say.

In Valsesia?

Not exactly news.

This time Luigi took a nice sip of whisky. Now his throat no longer burned. He looked for cigarettes and turned his back to the two, who after a while left them alone.

And how does he take them out? Alfredo whispered.

With his thumb, Luigi made a cut-throat motion.

Stray dogs?

No, no. The one today was a guard dog.

No kidding.

A real beast. Shepherds, guard dogs.

Dogs with owners.

If that's how you see it.

He's the one who sees it that way.

He who?

Alfredo unsheathed his skewed smile. He was wearing a denim tank top and a thick shirt whose buttons he undid. He leaned towards his brother, as if to show him something secret, and freed his left shoulder from the sleeve: he had a wolf's head tattooed on his arm. Shredded muscles, Luigi noticed. Who knows if he'd been lifting weights or if they'd come from cutting down trees? The wolf's muzzle stretched across Alfredo's bicep, the eyes stared from his deltoid, ears finishing under his tank top. Not one of those mangy wolves that roamed the Alps, skinny and cautious like thieves. A wolf from the Far North, thick fur and proud gaze, staring at him from his brother's arm.

Look at that, Luigi said. Nice work.

You know who did it for me?

Who?

An Indian woman.

You have Indians in Canada?

Still a few.

So he's the one with something against dogs with owners.

Alfredo slipped his arm back into his sleeve. He didn't fasten the buttons on his shirt. He left it open, adjusted himself on the stool and stroked his mug with a sly look.

He said: Wanna bet?

What?

I say it's a wolf.

Luigi thought: this is gonna take a while. He smelled the stench again of the dead dog that had infested his Defender all afternoon. He looked for the whisky and all he found was the bottom of the glass.

*

He woke up on a torn sofa, wrapped in a blanket, and the first smell that reached his nose was that of the wood stove burning. The smell of childhood. He spotted the old refrigerator, the sink, the window overlooking the woods. He sat up and his head spun like a small boat in the waves. It was his father's house, yes. Fontana Fredda. The thought came back to him that at some point in the night he had emerged from the alcohol with a glimmer of the solution. There was a coffee pot on the stove, and mouse droppings on the wooden floor. Nothing in there had been touched in ages. The blanket smelled like mould and that mouse had put a hole in it, finding nothing else to eat. Great fucking idea, he thought. In his mouth he had an ashtray drowned in rancid beer. He dragged himself towards the bathroom to get himself together.

Outside, the November pastures were scorched by frost. Only a finger of snow in the shadow of the drystone walls and at the bottom of the irrigation canals. The clouds caressed the woods, fraying into puffs between the trees. Around the house, more sky than earth.

Luigi filled his lungs with that air. He took a sip of his father's coffee: after a year in a jar it still had some flavour. He saw the Suzuki parked and Alfredo sitting on the bench against the wall. He looked like he'd never gone to sleep. Wrapped in a blanket, he smoked, staring at the two trees next to the house. A larch and a fir, thirty-seven and thirty-five years old: the old man had planted them when they were born. At 1,800 metres they grew slowly; now they were just a little higher than the roof.

Luigi came closer, but didn't sit down. Too much intimacy that night.

Alfredo coughed. He spat out a gob of phlegm

and said: How come your wife doesn't want me in the house?

You're wrong.

I'm always the one who's wrong.

She's pregnant.

You told me.

He didn't remember telling him. Dense blackout from the second bar on. Anyway, he could believe what he wanted. He took a sip of coffee and looked at the larch: it had recently lost the needles that were now scattered on the ground, the colour of copper. It was growing straight, freed from the lower branches and looking for the light above. The fir tree, on the other hand, was thick with dark needles, the trunk hidden by foliage. The old man must have thought about the distance at which to plant them: at that age the branches of the two trees were touching each other. In a little while they would start to intertwine.

Luigi said: The notary appointment is tomorrow morning in Varallo.

Ugh, Alfredo said.

Maybe tonight I'll get you a room there.

That way I won't bail.

You got it.

But first, can you quench my curiosity?

Why not.

Can you explain to me what you plan to do with this hole?

Luigi looked up at the house. The attic of perforated bricks, which no one had bothered to plaster. The crooked gutters, the metal sheets that patched the roof. It had always been like this, for as long as he could remember.

Me and Betta are fixing to live here, he said.

In Fontana Fredda?

With the little girl, we need a bigger house. And she's tired of living down there.

She wants to live here?

I mean, check out the sky. Isn't it better than down there in the dark?

The whole valley below was still in the shade. There was snow on the distant ridges and tattered clouds in the gullies. The smell of fire and stables and dry hay.

You're crazy, Alfredo said.

So be it.

A girl, you said?

Betta's sure of it.

If that's what she says.

Luigi went to put the cup down and those three steps there made him feel seasick again. But he had to wake up because he was going on duty soon. He checked the pockets of his jacket and found his wallet, a crumpled pack of cigarettes, loose change and the house keys, but not those of the Suzuki. He looked up and down the sofa, then went out again to his brother, ashamed.

The keys to the truck?

They're in the truck.

Right. Are you coming with me?

No. I'll stay around here a bit.

You sure?

It's still my house, or am I wrong? At least for today.

And again, from one moment to the next, he felt a tenderness towards Fredo. Maybe he didn't get up from that bench because he couldn't stay on his feet, but he never let go of the tough-guy pose.

Luigi said: If you want to take something, go ahead.

Like?

I don't know, a memento.

Of this house? I'd just as soon torch it.

Well, please don't torch it, not today.

He got in the car. The keys were in the ignition, and he didn't want to think about which of them had driven up there. He started the engine and turned on the heat. He looked in the mirror, checked that his brother couldn't see, then bent down to open the glove compartment. Bending over made him want to puke, but the pistol was still there.

*

When he was almost at the command post, he heard the blades of a helicopter, looked up through the windscreen and saw it flying over the valley. It had a load on the winch that looked like an animal to him at that moment. He turned at the traffic light, entered the parking lot and found the deputy inspector with his nose in the air, next to the muddy pick-up of a group of hunters. The helicopter was descending. Luigi observed it against the sky: the shiny cockpit, the taut steel cable, and a large deer hanging by its hind legs, its forelegs stiff up front, rack swaying. When it was twenty metres from the ground, the wind from the blades swept the dry leaves from the car park. The deputy gestured to the pilot to help him centre the bed of the truck, and as the deer came down Luigi saw that it was already gutted. Its belly was open up to the sternum. The hunters placed its head in a corner, antlers sticking out from one side of the bed. They unhooked the winch; the animal collapsed and settled, and within seconds the helicopter was already an insect in the distance.

Then they could relax and celebrate. The lucky one was the youngest of the three, his face smooth as a child's above his camouflage, and the one patting him hard on the back could have been his father. Luigi looked at the animal's antlers: the tips white and worn from life in the woods; he counted eight points on each side. A fully developed male who that morning at dawn was lusting for females in love and didn't even notice who had him in their sights.

Hassles of the day: another dead dog, and the analyses of the river water had arrived. A quantity of chemical solvents that could even melt stones was poisoning the Sesia, well before it reached the rice fields.

In the office, the deputy was registering the kill. One of the hunters said: So, have you caught the dog-killer?

Not yet, Luigi said.

How you planning to deal with it?

Maybe it'll switch valleys.

We'll put a posse together and take care of it ourselves.

In a helicopter?

Look, chief, you didn't see what a beast that was? Either that, or we had to cut him to pieces to get him down.

And how much did that toy cost you?

Nothing.

Nothing?

A client owes me a favour.

I'd say he deserves a salami or two.

The conversation was stimulating, but it was the chief inspector who interrupted it. Inspectress, actually, even though she would take offense at being called that. They had sent her six months ago, and the irony of being bossed around by a woman wore off after a week. She looked out and said: Balma, can you come here for a second?

Luigi ran his tongue over his gums, which he found to be sandy. He went over to where a 1:25,000 map was lying on his boss's desk. One glance was enough for him to recognise Fontana Fredda. On that Military Geographic Institute map, the route of the new ski lift was marked, which they would begin building in the spring. He hadn't seen it with his own eyes yet. The project included a chair-lift, a departure and arrival station, a service road, three ski slopes. They'd been talking about it for a long time, up in the Region offices. The integrated tourism development plan. But for the moment they were just pen strokes some surveyor had drawn.

You're from these parts, aren't you? the chief said.

I was born there.

And you go back?

Sometimes, on Sundays.

So tell me what kind of woods we have here.

The inspector indicated the land crossed by the development. It was designed by surveyors and financed by politicians, but to deforest it you still had to go through the Forestry Department. Luigi approached the map. He squinted and the boss noticed.

You want these? she said, handing him her reading glasses.

Luigi put them on. He felt like an idiot with those glasses on his nose, but he could see the elevation lines again. He placed his finger to the left of the chairlift and said: This is called Fontana Fredda Wood. It's a natural forest, mixed fir and larch. The oldest plants must be two hundred years old. Here it's all private property.

Owners?

Go figure. Twenty different heirs living in France and Belgium. Except when you want to cut a plant, then someone always shows up and says *that there is mine.*

Then he pointed to the woods to the right of the chairlift, where the main slope passed. Two wide curves were drawn for the pleasure of future skiers. He said: Whereas this is the Burnt Wood. There was a fire at the beginning of the century. Here it's consortium property. They replanted the larch to make it a grazing forest, but the last time anything grazed there was when I was a kid.

The chief inspector smiled. She was probably imagining Agent Balma as a child.

Who calls it Burnt Wood?

Well, maybe only me by now.

What's the population of Fontana Fredda?

Seven. That is, if no one died today.

Well, things'll be changing up there a little soon enough.

Let's hope.

It was the hangover that made him sentimental. And also this woman, in whom he confided instinctively. He pointed to the arrival station of the chairlift, high up, near the stream, and said: My father took me here to set traps.

Traps?

Snares and footholds.

What'd you catch?

Foxes. Martens. Anything.

He was a poacher?

Like everyone. With one skin we could get by for a week.

You don't have any of those traps left, do you?

No, I put them away.

I'll pretend I believe you. And which house is yours?

This one, Luigi said. He placed his index finger on a dot in the middle of the pastures. There it was, high and isolated, his father's house. Even at Fontana Fredda he hadn't been able to live close to the others and built it outside, right on the edge of the piste that wasn't there yet.

*

He passed by the Croce Bianca just before one o'clock, the time when the workers were already at the café and some truck drivers were still coming in, attracted by the handwritten sign displayed on the road. Fixed menu – first course, second course, side dish, coffee – 9,000 lira. Today's special: polenta and roe deer, tagliatelle with wild game ragú, baked trout with potatoes. The table near the window was free and he went to sit there, even though he wasn't hungry, and if he had been, would have lost his appetite anyway, knowing what was in those trout. Not that the deer drank their water on Mars. He took a piece of bread from the basket, more to chew something than anything else, and looked at the sparse autumn traffic in front of the restaurant. He tried to remember what they had done last night. He remembered different bars and his brother's wolf that flashed every now and then, until he had completely taken off his shirt and stayed in his tank top. What had they talked about? The old man's death, for sure. About how it had gone and what he looked like and how they took him away. Alfredo knew nothing about the ski slope and Luigi was careful not to tell him. Now he wondered if he was ripping him off. No, he wasn't ripping him off. Fredo hadn't even come back for the funeral. If he had wanted to cheat him, he would have left him there in Canada and kept the house, instead of offering him five million for half that hole. It was money raining down from the sky – he just had to come and get it. Luigi felt, if not honest, at least as honest as he could be.

Fires: that's what he'd talked about at one point. In Canada, even fires were huge. Whereas in Valsesia everything was small, and he watched a tractor turning off the country road into a dirt one between the fields, the no-entry sign perforated by a bullet hole.

If they don't die, then you'll see them again, said Elisabetta.

Right, Luigi said.

He found her by far the most beautiful thing of that day: even with the 'Campari Soda' apron on and the order pad in her hand. He reached out and caressed her hip, ever so slightly, because he knew she didn't want any sweet nothings in there. Elisabetta didn't return the caress.

What can I bring you?

How do you do those potatoes?

Roasted.

Potatoes then.

And?

A beer.

Well, well, breakfast of champions.

She wrote potatoes in her notepad and cleared the other setting at the table. He watched her take the order to the kitchen, go to the bar tap to pour his beer, then back to the kitchen to collect her plate. After a night with his brother, it seemed incredible to him to have a wife like that. The workers x-rayed her every time she passed by.

Elisabetta served it and sat down in front of him.

She said: Will I see you tonight?

Luigi shrugged his shoulders.

I have to keep an eye on my brother till tomorrow. You know how he is.

Where did you leave him?

Fontana Fredda. If he hasn't already come down on foot.

You slept up there?

I guess you could call it sleep . . .

Don't you think about me worrying?

She unwittingly raised her voice, and some people started looking at them. Luigi kept silent, stretched out a hand to the centre of the table.

He opened it, as if imploring her. She looked at it, somewhat defiant, then gave up and offered him hers. He squeezed it and said he was sorry, and she said she wasn't able to sulk with him.

You have a lot to do today?

The usual. Dead dogs to be collected and road checks.

He felt her grip tighten. Elisabetta's hand was a little sweaty, like when she got upset.

She said: I saw them, you know.

Who?

The dogs.

What dogs?

It wasn't just one dog. There were two of them.

Where did you see them?

At the river.

At the river?

Luigi straightened up in his chair. He held her hand and paid close attention.

She said: This morning I got scared because you hadn't come back. So I went there, to our old spot. I go there when I need to calm down. I went into the water and at one point I saw these two dogs looking at me.

Luigi imagined his wife, pregnant, entering the

freezing and polluted waters of the Sesia. How long had she been doing it? He preferred to address the other question, which seemed simpler to him.

What were the two dogs like?

One was a female. Smaller, white. The male was big and grey. She had a collar; he didn't.

Could it have been a wolf?

I don't know.

A bell rang in the kitchen and Elisabetta turned around. Coming, she said. She let go of Luigi's hand.

What do you mean, you don't know?

I mean, how do you know it's a wolf?

You know, believe me.

Does that change much?

You bet it does.

She thought about it. She tried to replay the scene while Luigi reflected. He told himself that dogs and wolves don't wander around together, not since the beginning of the world. And wolves roam at night, dogs during the day. Unless everything was now as skewed as flying deer.

I think it was a dog, she said.

Better, he said.

I have to go.

Elisabetta stood up. She gave him a quick stroke

of the shoulder. Luigi's throat was parched but he waited until he was alone to take the glass. Then he downed half of it in one gulp. The beer went straight to where it was needed.

*

It was small, his valley, and yet there were still places he had never seen. Having come down from the berm, he let the man go ahead and looked at the landscape of poplars and birches, a basin where the Sesia made a bend between the gravel banks shaped by the current. Now that it was dry, the river branched out, creating islands and beaches. It occurred to him that ten years earlier he used to take Elisabetta here for a swim, but there was a season in life for swimming in the river. Who knows why it passed? Then came the season of children, of houses to buy and renovate, of a regular pay cheque. Here and there a crust of snow covered the bank, and in the snow, following the man, Luigi found the blood of that day.

The Rottweiler had its throat torn up, like the other dogs. But unlike the others, he had put up a fight and had visible wounds on his shoulders and muzzle. His mouth was also full of blood, which may or may not have been his: this dog could have bitten his killer. The fight took place in a few metres of loose snow. Short and violent, between the gurgling water and the birches.

Luigi picked up the collar ripped off by the bite. It must have taken a lot of strength to break the leather.

Did you see what happened? he asked.

No, the guy said. We got here late.

What were you two doing here, walking with this big dog?

Doing what you guys don't.

He was a man who had been crying, and Luigi didn't want to aggravate it. He left him there, with his dead dog, and followed the other's footprints as they walked away into the snow. He went upriver for a while, piecing together the tracks he read: the dog was medium-sized, not a giant. He was bleeding and limping. They had to thank the Rottweiler who bit the dust but made his job easier. After a hundred metres, some smaller footprints joined the first ones, and Luigi thought back to Elisabetta's story. This was the white female. The female's footsteps followed those of the male and the blood he left behind. Until they both waded towards the other bank and Luigi stopped to look ahead.

The river upstream hollowed into the valley, narrowed into torrents. The banks became steep and no longer offered many escape routes. It was hard for a wounded animal. A good hunter wouldn't have much trouble getting him out of there.

*

While driving down the road, he saw a motorbike missing its number plates parked outside a bar. His foot moved on its own to the brake pedal. It was the white and red Fantic dirt bike they used as boys in the fields, out of commission for years in the old man's stable. He had tried, a few times, to clean the carburettor and change the spark plug, but he had never been much of a mechanic. It was Fredo who had the touch. Luigi had no desire, but he had to pull over, get out of the car, take a deep breath and go into that fucking bar.

Oh, the good brother, someone said.

And someone else: I told you he was coming.

He recognised the guy they called Johnny

standing at the bar with his elbows set firm. Next to him, none other than René delle Piode. Alfredo closed off the line-up in front of a glass of Baileys: he had to admit, he was still in shape, his brother was. At four in the afternoon, he might not have been in his tank top, but he was walking around with a hatchet in his belt.

You resurrected the Fantic, he said.

You're the one who said take a memento.

Yeah, but you don't have any plates.

Only till tomorrow. Just enough time to get to the notary, eh?

Alfredo winked at him and the two others grinned. There was a quip Luigi pretended not to hear.

He said: You wanna come with me for a second to talk?

Sure.

He took him out the service exit, a door with a fly curtain. They found themselves in a country courtyard: in front of the place there was an Irish pub sign with the Guinness logo, out back was a chicken coop, two bags of feed, and the old latrine that still served as a toilet for the bar.

So, you can't just lie low for a couple of days? Luigi said. What are you doing with that hatchet?

I'm kinda fond of it, Alfredo said.

You can't go around like that. You'll get into trouble.

You thought I wouldn't find out about the ski slope?

What ski slope?

You know what I'm talking about.

They told you?

The good brother!

Alfredo burst out laughing. Luigi realised his heart was racing. He would have been a terrible poker player, incapable of bluffing. He reached for cigarettes, tapped the pack on the back of his hand, and two popped out.

Alfredo took one and put it between his lips. He enjoyed that moment of payback, the blush on his brother's face. Then he said: Look, I don't care, you can keep the house. You deserve it. I'm only bummed that you bullshitted me.

What bullshit?

What do you really want to do with it? A little bar on the slopes? Or are you gonna resell it right away?

I'm not selling it. Me and Betta are gonna live there.

And then?

I still don't know.

Yeah, I can see you. A nice bar on the slope. You'll get it together.

Luigi gave him a light and looked at his face. In the flame of the lighter, Fredo had a shiny forehead and dilated pupils. Who knows how long he'd been drinking – he hadn't stopped since the night before. Or maybe from the one before that.

You found your old buddies again, Luigi said.

The ones who aren't dead.

Plans for tonight?

You're still worried. Don't fret, I'll be there at your notary's.

You don't want me to take you to a hotel?

No.

They smoked. Agent Balma now felt completely disarmed. Four in the afternoon, his brother drunk for two days, another November night falling. A part of him just wanted to take off his uniform and hang out at the bar with those three.

You know what I want, though? Alfredo said.

What?

A nice hug from my brother. Or even a fistfight, you choose. But something real.

Fredo stared at him with those boozy eyes – skewed, but not ferocious. Eyes of a man more honest than himself. Luckily, at that moment, a guy came out to piss and Luigi was able to look away.

*

That evening he had a real cop's shift, with the deputy inspector stopping cars at the Romagnano toll booth. Not bad for someone who'd been driving drunk all night. But there at the motorway exit they weren't looking for drunks, they were looking for toxic waste that was poisoning the river: unless it rained from the sky, it had to come from somewhere.

A truck passed the toll booth, carrying construction site refuse and the deputy flashed him the warning sign. He braked with a hiss, downshifted, pulled up behind the Defender like a docile pachyderm. He was coming from the Milan region, headed for the landfill. They stopped a lot of them like this: in the city they demolished the factories and tons of rubble arrived in the valleys to be disposed of. While the deputy checked the cabin,

Luigi climbed onto the bed from the side rail. He turned on the torch, put it in his mouth and shined it on the load. Concrete, brick, conglomerate, as far as he could see, all crushed into a grey mixture, along with the substances absorbed over decades of production. He put on gloves to fill three plastic bags, which he would then label and send to the lab. The rubble would wind up in the valley's quarries that had been exhausted and turned into land-fills; the gravel and sand went back to where they came from, just a little dirtier than before, like the unemployed workers in front of their drinks. Luigi jumped down from the bed, put the samples away, and they let the poor truck driver dying of sleep-lessness go.

At seven, the Defender's radio crackled. The deputy answered – it was the Alagna Carabinieri asking for support. Over in the upper valley, they had a seriously injured man lying on the floor of a bar with his skull smashed in. Alive, at least for the moment. They were taking him away in code red. The attacker was a man around forty, identity unknown, spotted fleeing on a motorcycle.

How long ago did he leave? the deputy asked.

About fifteen minutes, the radio said.

The number plate?

No number plate. It was a red-and-white moto-cross bike.

What was the weapon?

A woodcutter's hatchet.

Christ, Luigi thought.

He got behind the wheel – there was no need to discuss anything: he left the toll booth, turned on the flashing light and took the back road, which cut across the plain in that stretch. On the straight-away, he accelerated to ninety kilometres an hour. There were sixty to Alagna. He knew each one of them and only needed half of them to get to Varallo before that dirt bike. There, the road branched off in too many directions to know which one he would take. But from Varallo upwards there was only one, a dead end: with a single checkpoint you controlled the whole valley.

A hatchet in the head, the deputy said, that's all that was missing.

You must not've been here back in the day.

Oh yeah? What's that, a traditional game.

More or less.

Driving fast forced simple thoughts on him. Let that pair of headlights pass, widen to the left, pass the truck, slip back in. Make sure they stop there, then go straight through the traffic lights. Serravalle, Borgosesia, the bridge over the river. And in the meantime: don't let him die, don't let him die. An attempted murder is not murder. If the hatchet didn't cut into him, he might just be injured. Fredo knew how to swing an axe. If he wanted to kill him, he would have killed him.

The Fantic came with no headlight, burned out for years. In the dark stretch just before Varallo, he whizzed past as if mocking them. His brother's face lit up for an instant: in the time it took the eye to send the image to the brain he had already passed. His foot slammed on the brake and his arm yanked the steering wheel down.

Is that it? the deputy said, holding on to the handle. Luigi didn't even answer him. He went into the meadow, swerved left and bounced back onto the road in the opposite direction. Once the moment was lost, he had two or three hundred metres to recover.

Now they were really brothers. Fredo ahead, low on the handlebars, hair in the wind, and Luigi with his foot on the accelerator and the flashing light on. Down in their valley, on a road they could have taken with their eyes closed. You wanted something real? Here you go: something real.

On the curves, the Fantic had an edge, but as the valley began to flatten the Defender gained ground. That wreck couldn't hit a hundred kilometres an hour. Now he had him in the cone of his headlights, he could make out Alfredo's back; and when Alfredo also felt the blue of the flashing light on him, he decided to change tack and veered right at the first clearing. Luigi followed him into a truck park, then onto the dirt road between two warehouses. Beyond the warehouses, in the middle of the fields, they entered the darkness.

How can he drive in the dark? he heard the deputy say.

He's so drunk he can see, Luigi thought with his mouth closed.

The dirt road ended at the edge of a thicket, again the scrub that ran along the river. It became a trail Alfredo could slip into, but Luigi was forced to stop. To the right and left he had the fields, in front of him that forest. Race over.

Shit, the deputy said.

But in the end, it was the excuse Luigi was waiting for to let him slip away. He turned on his high beams and still managed to glimpse his brother disappearing into the trees. Ciao, Fredo. That was the last time he would see him, he thought, then shifted into reverse to go back to the command post.

*

He was sitting over beer and whisky again that night when he remembered the fires Alfredo had told him about. In who knows which of the valley's bars, or maybe while driving, by then in that place beyond the binge, a place of absolute presence and lucidity, only in another dimension. It was there that you could drive in the dark. And while his brother was telling the story, he could see: he saw the Canadian forest in flames, saw it burning throughout the autumn, until the snow came to cover the fire. Heavy snow from November to April. A six-month winter, up in the north. But even all that snow just suffocated the fire without snuffing it, Fredo had said, and do you know why? Because the fire had entered so deep that the ground itself was burning, that humus of peat, leaves, rotten wood, two or three metres deep under the forest, had become embers under the ash. Asleep, but not completely extinguished. Luigi could see it pulsate very slowly:

and in the state he was in he saw that the forest was him, the fire was within; the snow was his marriage. It was Elisabetta's white skin and the peace she gave him. Then his brother told him about the thaw, which up there in Canada didn't come until late May. Then the embers returned to the surface, black, damp, apparently dead. But they weren't dead. Till one day the spring wind rose. Phew! Fredo said, blowing on him and setting everything on fire.

Passing the Winter

My brother went to work and left me alone in the house where our father killed himself a year ago. I wasn't there at the time. I was in the woods of British Columbia chopping trees six days a week. One Sunday I get back to the city and my brother calls me. He's been trying to get me for a while: he says Pops shot himself in the head with his trusty 12-calibre rifle after they discovered cancer in some vital organ while in the hospital. Liver, I think. Or maybe the pancreas, I don't remember. Anyway, I stood there imagining it for a second. I imagined Pops taking the rifle, loading it, turning it around in his hand, sticking it under his chin. Where did it happen? I asked. In the meadow in front of the house, my brother said. Did you find him? No, he said, my wife did. We had the funeral yesterday; I've been calling you for four days.

A year ago, I hadn't come back – what was the point, anyway? – but since then my brother started calling me, as if he'd just remembered he was the older brother. How are you doing? he asked me. Great, I said. And then a minute of silence between Valsesia and British Columbia, as wide as the ocean in between. Until he spat it out and offered to buy my half of the house, which I didn't even think would be worth anything. Five million, minus the price of the plane ticket, for a holiday in the valley and a signature at the notary.

Here in the yard there are these two trees that the old man had planted when we were born. Both in the autumn, '57 and '59. Autumn is supposed to be a good time to have children, and it certainly is for transplanting trees. It's when the growing season ends and tearing them out of the ground is less of a hassle for them. Then they sleep, in their own way, so they have the whole winter to recover, and if it snows, it's even better. It's like being under the covers. God willing, in spring they wake up and begin to suck from the roots, sprout new leaves, and settle in where they weren't born but now they have to live. What I don't know, and what I never asked the old man, is why back then he chose a larch for my brother and a fir for me. We were too young for him to see anything in us, so maybe it was just a gut feeling on his part. Or who knows, a blessing. You, larch, are destined to grow in the sun, to rise to the heights, hard and fragile, and sway in the wind. You, fir tree, on the other hand, will grow darkly in the shade, but strong and resilient, protected by needles even in winter, adapted to the cold. That's me.

I'm sure my brother's already pinched the rifle, so I wander around that hovel looking for something to drink. Down in the cellar there isn't a drop of anything left – only potatoes that have sprouted. I open the wardrobe, the fridge, the cupboards, until I find a half-bottle of grappa inside a pot. Who was Pops hiding it from? I rinse a dusty cup in the sink, pour some in the coffee, but I don't smell any alcohol, as if the grappa has lost its proof. I smell the bottle, taste it. It's still the same, but seems evaporated or watered down. I pour a long shot into my coffee. The coffee turns strong, just like I need this morning. I throw a log into the stove and wonder who chopped this wood: has it been here for a year or does my brother come every now and then to warm the place up? And the potatoes? I think of Pops pulling up potatoes just before shooting himself. Must've been during that period.

I look outside. The sun melts the frost in the field. Memories also soften with time. Now that he's gone, I've forgotten about many other things and only remember him as a sad man. Papa grew sad together with this place. In Canada you recognise First Nation houses because they often have broken-down cars in the yard, a camper trailer where people can go get drunk, old tyres, two or three children in dirty clothes. They used to be wolves, then they became stray dogs. There's nothing you can give them in exchange for what they lost: no reserve as big as Valsesia, no unlimited hunting licence. Something in them has died forever. Papa was just like that: people were leaving Fontana Fredda and he was the one being abandoned, a piece of his heart bolted shut and left in the frozen cold, weeds growing in the wild fields of his spirit.

I pour myself another cup of coffee and grappa. I go outside around the back to the stable. There I find the traps for the foxes and the snowshoes we'd put on to go out and set them up. The baler Pops used to curse at and the broken fridge where he kept screws and nails. I find the chainsaw, too, the same old Stihl: except that a mouse has managed to gnaw the tank cap away and die inside it. Attracted by the smell of oil, it drowned in the petrol. So I take one of the hatchets hanging on the wall – after all, that's how it should be done – and I go back outside, put my cup on a block of wood, spit into the palms of my hands and start whaling on that tree.

I don't notice that while I'm hacking and hewing someone comes my way; it's old Gemma passing by with a wheelbarrow full of manure.

Alfredo, she says, and I stop for a moment. I look at her. She puts down the wheelbarrow. You're back?

Just for today, Gemma, I say.

What are you doing?

Wood for the winter.

Your father put that plant in.

I don't answer her any more and keep working. It's not that big a trunk. Thirty-five years, thirty-five growth rings, thin years and thick years, fortune and misfortune. I pick up the pace, warm up, the wood is soft and the blade is sharp. A few minutes and I deliver the final blow. Gemma is still there

69

watching when the fir tips over and goes down, without making much noise.

*

It was to avoid ending up like that mouse that, at the age of sixteen, I left my old man and went to work on construction sites. First as a labourer, then I found René who taught me how to lay slate for roofs. *Piode*, we call the slabs in these parts. Today people cook steaks on them, but once upon a time they used them to cover the roofs of their houses, and here the traditional houses are protected by the fine arts agency, so work was guaranteed. The slabs need to be changed from time to time. Nobody knows how to do it any more. Slate is a schistose rock, which means that it flakes off into pieces, and the thinner and lighter the slabs – which is what's needed to stay on a roof – the more fragile they are, and they crack like nothing. With René, we spent eight months of the year on the roofs, half naked, roasted by the sun. From March to November, more or less. I gave him a hand and in the meantime learned how to choose the stone, shape it with the hammer, drill two holes for nails, all without shattering it. It was a job that

I liked, but then there were the other four months, those on the ground. René had his own ways of spending the winter, mostly hunting and going to bars. And I trailed behind him, like a good brave.

I go down to the valley like on one of those mornings. I hang the hatchet on my belt and start the motorbike I used back then. When I was twenty, the cops turned a blind eye to the number plate: I was a worker going to work. Today, though, I'm an emigrant who's come home, so I stop at Sporting even though it's November; the tennis court is covered by a plastic tarpaulin and in the middle of the tarp a large puddle reflects the sky.

It's not even ten in the morning, but who do I find there at the counter with a glass of white in front of his muzzle? Seems like yesterday.

Oh Fredo, René says, they let you out?

I see there's vintage furniture here, I say.

Nice sidearm you got there, might need a permit for that.

Not as nice as yours.

We toast to friendship and, as happens in these parts, in no time we go from two to three of us, and then from three to four. I don't know the third one. The fourth, called Johnny, is someone I wound up together with at the police station on Christmas '85. One evening we smashed up a disco and a few chairs across the backs of some tourists, Milanese who came up here skiing and then spent their holiday in the hospital. We couldn't stand them, or maybe some girls were involved. Who can remember? They took us in. During the night, trying to explain my reasons to the marshal, I told him that they came from Milan and I was from Fontana Fredda, a town of twenty souls at 1,800 metres above sea level, and that's how I got stuck with my nickname.

Eighteen Hundred's here! he says.

Hey, Johnny, I say.

Everyone's working, eh?

Someone's got to do it, René says.

Johnny has a drink with us and in the meantime starts yakking about some hunting trip, let's call it that, he heard about. Set for earlier in the morning, apparently, not far from here. He says stuff and doesn't say anything and I don't know who he's bullshitting, which usually means you're the one being bullshitted. Then I remember the dead dogs and catch the drift. I ask: What hunt are you talking about, Johnny? Wolf hunting?

Or dog, says the one whose name I didn't get.

Whatever it is or isn't, ten minutes later the four of us are in someone's truck, headed somewhere. The day is grey and electrifying. Typical autumn morning in my valley.

*

After Fior di Roccia, we leave the provincial road. We take a dirt road that goes downhill. I understand where we're going and when I glimpse the water my heart aches. Once you've got used to the rivers in Canada, once you've cut down trees along the Fraser or fished for salmon in the Kootenai, seeing the Sesia again after seven years kicks up a quaint fondness – it's a river for kids. As we go up it, I remember when Pops used to take us to catch trout. He put a piece of carbide, the kind that was once used in acetylene lamps, in a jar; he made a hole in the lid and threw it into a pool. When the carbide came into contact with water, it produced acetylene, and the jar exploded. The old man didn't do it for sport: he would send us to sell the trout in the surrounding restaurants, and they willingly bought them from us. Just like they bought chamois or ibex those rare times he bagged one.

Today there's no water. It barely reaches the

bed as we wade. I check for a fin flicker, a shadow slipping away. If I were a trout, I would be right there, in that darkest, deepest hole. We follow a tyre track, we get tossed around a bit more, until we find two off-road vehicles parked among the branches and we go down too, but seeing the river again makes me sad.

Johnny and the other guy continue on foot in search of the hunters. I tell them I'll stay and watch the truck. René doesn't feel like walking around, and once they've left, he rummages in the back, opens a case from the wine co-op cellar, takes out a bottle and a screwdriver from the toolbox under the seat. I see it's a tried-and-true method.

Wouldn't it be quicker to keep a corkscrew? I ask.

I always forget, he says.

There's a little wind on the riverbed and it makes me want to light a fire. In front of the cars there's a birch tree lying on the ground, withered. I take the axe from my belt, cut branches and twigs and pile them against the trunk, on the sand. I hear René uncorking. Using the hatchet as a plane, I strip the white bark, which comes off in thin curls that fall to the side. I gather a handful, place it under the twigs and set it on fire with the lighter. A wisp of smoke rises, a small flame. Then the twigs begin to crackle, and René comes to hand me the bottle.

So, how's Canada? he says.

Too big, I say.

You got a lady?

Get outta here.

No girls in Canada?

Hardly any. If you need to, you go into the city.

Well, the whole world is a village.

I take a nice sip of Gattinara, feel it going down to warm my stomach, watch the fire pick up strength. No, the whole world is not a village. I say: Once I wanted to see where Canada ended. I laid out a mattress in the bed of the truck and started driving north. That's how they travel there, you know.

Nice, René says.

I took a road called the Klondike Highway. Two thousand klicks and change to Dawson City. Nothing but lakes, woods, bears and moose who don't even look at you when you pass.

The Klondike, isn't that in Alaska?

No, it's in Canada. But it doesn't just finish in Dawson, another road starts there, the Dempster. All dirt. Another seven hundred klicks of potholes and mud straight up north. Halfway, you cross the Arctic Circle.

Seven hundred kilometres of dirt road? René says.

That's right.

And what's the Arctic Circle like?

Tundra. It's not a real forest, just these dwarf trees. Moss. Big valleys and gas pumps. When you come across a river, you wait for the ferry to take you to the other side.

I pass him the bottle. René takes a sip without dropping his eyes from me. He wants to know where Canada ends.

And you know what's there at the end of all that road? A place. Inuvik, it's called. You can't believe anyone lives up there. The houses are on stilts built on permafrost. And in front there's the Arctic Ocean, and oil wells planted in the middle of the sea.

Stilts?

Yeah. The post office is a stilt house, the church is a stilt house and the bar is a stilt house. I went inside for a drink once. End of Canada.

René doesn't say anything any more, maybe because he's trying to imagine it. Or maybe he's trying to remember the furthest place from home he's ever been to: Ibiza, I think. We pass the bottle around. I'm reminded of those days on the Dempster when it never got dark. It was summer, even if up there it's only summer in name, and the sun would sink towards the north with this endless sunset, hanging on the horizon for hours. Until it became a dawn and the sun rose again. I spent a night in the bed of the pickup looking at the sky from my sleeping bag, and never like that time did I think: this world doesn't really give a shit about us. Definitely not about me.

René drinks and stares into the fire. I see movement along the river.

They didn't get him, I say.

What? he says, snapping out of it.

The wolf. They didn't get him – look.

The hunters come down from the woods with their camouflage and rifles. A couple of dogs on leashes. One is talking loudly, slipping a curse into every sentence. I guess that's enough for this morning – now we can go back and eat.

*

Trattoria Alpina da Anna. The chamois salami consoles the hunters. The valley's good red loosens Johnny's tongue.

Eighteen Hundred, he says, what do you think? Wolf or dog?

For me, it's a wolf, I say.

So where is he moseying on up to?

Back home.

Listen up, listen up! he yells. Eighteen Hundred has a theory.

C'mon, don't bust his balls, René says.

Am I busting your balls?

No, not at all.

So, where's his home?

I point to the ceiling with my eyes. Johnny follows my gaze.

Upstairs? he says.

Right there.

And what should we do about it?

Let him go.

He looks at me. I look at him. I think it's written on my face that yes, he's busting my balls. So he chooses to play it safe and turns towards the table to bust someone else's.

René was telling me something that caught my interest. Go ahead, René, I say.

He bites the salami with his molars. He lost his incisors when he was young, opening beers with his teeth. He says: The Region puts the money in, it's not a private company. For the Region it raises land value. For us, we get guaranteed jobs. It starts with a chairlift, but then who knows.

How many people are they hiring?

At the chairlift, about ten. Machinists. Snowcat operators. The guy who gives you his hand to get off the lift. But then calculate the rentals, the ticket office. You need at least one bar, right?

If not two.

There you go. What's that, thirty jobs?

In Fontana Fredda!

Why not? Look at Cervinia. You know what was there before?

No, I say.

It was a meadow with two mountain pastures and a small church. Only they made a mistake there, they sold everything to outsiders. They thought they were getting a deal – you know how it is. They sold the land at pasture prices and then ended up with five-star hotels.

Not a bargain.

No, not by a long shot.

I look outside. I look at the U that the valley makes at this point, a beautiful curve of erosion covered by the woods, and I understand that my brother is trying to pull a fast one on me. Five million for a house on the ski slopes? At a guess, in a year he can sell it for fifty. But it's only right, I suppose. He stayed, I didn't. It wasn't me who took Pops to the hospital. I wasn't there when they told him about the cancer, and I didn't bring him home afterwards. I didn't have to tell him: you know, Papa, maybe they're wrong. I didn't find him in the yard with his head blown to bits.

I say: Back in the day, we used to kick the skiers' asses.

Now we're helping them onto the chairlift, says René.

I can't see me doing that, bro.

I don't know. You know what they say in these situations.

What do they say?

Cherchez la femme.

*

One time I even went out with her – my brother's wife. It was before she got together with him. I remember the year because I'd just got my driving licence: 1978. It's August, she's a girl who comes here on holiday. René and I are fixing the roof of her parents' house, one of those old log houses that the Milanese buy. I meet her on the construction site and invite her out. It seems like a miracle that she says yes. I ask René to borrow his car so I can take her out. I'm eighteen and she's sixteen, more or less. I thought about going to the campsite where they play music and dance, but that morning I wake up and it's pouring. No roofs with René. I stay at home looking out of the window and spend the day saying: Now it'll stop, it can't come down in buckets for much longer. Instead, it gets worse, and I get angrier. It's Valsesia, the valley has something against me and, in the evening, I decide to challenge it. I get cocky and go to pick the girl up. I still remember her on the balcony: Are you sure? she says. Me with my elbow out of the window: We're in Valsesia. Look at what a beautiful night it is. She runs to the car and that stretch is all she needs to have a shower.

You don't know what that river can become after just one day of heavy rain. At the first bridge I notice it: the water is no longer grey from the glacier but mud brown, making whirlpools against the pylons where it sends the trunks it pulls down crashing into it. You can hear the sound of rocks clonking together underwater. Okay, I'm only eighteen, but at this point I should understand that it's time to back off. Instead, I keep going, managing to cross the bridge just before they close it. Genius, Fredo. Further up, the road is cut off by a landslide. The bridge is now closed, so the rescue crews send us to a hotel where those from the campsite are taking refuge. It's exactly the campsite where I wanted to take the girl dancing: swept away by the Sesia, caravan trailers and all. We spend the night at the refuge camp, her terrified parents looking for her. In the morning, the rescue crews take her home and we both understand that our story was not born under a lucky star.

*

I get them to tell me where she works now. After lunch, I say goodbye to my companions and go down on my dirt bike to the Croce Bianca. It's snowing when I leave, drizzling when I get there. I feel neither one nor the other and stop at the back of the restaurant where there's the veranda with foosball and plastic tables and the ice cream sign, a picture of distant summers. It seems like just the place where someone like me can wait. I walk out onto the veranda, lean on the foosball table. The awning can't keep the rain out and the cigarette butts drown in the ashtrays. Dry leaves rot on the deck: I recognise their shape and look at the large maple that shades the courtyard in summer. It wouldn't have done anything for me years ago. There are no maples in Fontana Fredda. Now I almost feel like I love them. You see how life drops you down in altitude: I used to be a fir tree, then I became a maple. I pick up one of those leaves and pin it on my jacket pocket.

Alfredo, a woman's voice says to me. I'm looking for it; it's coming from beyond a small window. She still has the red hair she had then. I think it's the bathroom window over there.

Signora Balma, I say. Pleasure.

What are you doing there?

I'm waiting.

It's raining on you, Alfredo.

I don't give a rat's ass about any rain.

My brother's wife looks at me. I know that look. She looks at the hatchet in my belt and the maple leaf on my breast pocket. She's trying to gauge how drunk I am.

I say: I just want to know one thing.

Tell me, she says.

Is it true you were the one who found the old man?

Yeah.

And what were you doing there?

Is that what you want to know?

That's it.

She sighs, tucks her hair behind her ear. She's beautiful, my brother's wife. She's more beautiful now than at sixteen.

She says: Every now and then I'd visit him. That Sunday we harvested the potatoes. Whenever I had time, I'd cook him something.

You and him alone?

Almost always. It was a pleasure for him.

Every how often?

Once or twice a week.

I'm sure it was a pleasure for him. I can imagine this woman at Pops's house, cooking on the stove. Him sitting on the sofa looking at her. No woman had entered that house since his mother had left, horizontal, thirty years ago. What do they say to each other? He tells her about the old days. When people still lived in Fontana Fredda. He lets her cook even if he isn't hungry; by now he's only thirsty. Something comes to mind.

So it was you who put the water in the grappa?

Yes, Alfredo.

He thought he'd hidden it well.

Guess not.

I suddenly realise that I should've never come back. Once you're done, you're done. I look at this woman, who somehow got to know all three of us. The daughter of the Milanese on holiday, who would've thought? It occurs to me that she's pregnant. She looks at this man, her husband's brother, and I'm sure of what she's hoping for: she's hoping that the bad brother will go away soon, from this deck and from their lives.

I say: Do you remember? The one time we went out together, you and me.

Of course I remember.

Where was it we went?

We went out to dance, but it was raining.

You remember what day it was?

7 August, 1978. It's written on the plaques.

I put my hand out, palm up. Two drops fall from the awning. I say: They don't make floods like they used to, eh?

Come inside for a coffee, Alfredo, c'mon.

Ciao, Signora Balma.

*

The light goes down. The sky becomes grey like
the slate roofs. Outside the Woodland, I watch
my brother drive away in his police four-by-four.
I smoke one of his cigarettes while the rear lights
drift off, along with his feelings of guilt and his
efforts to keep on the straight and narrow. He even
uses the blinker to turn.

He's no saint, my brother, but look at us. A fir
and a larch. Dad understood everything. We both
took after him. We've known it since we were
children, except that my brother got one half and I
got the other, like with the house.

Tomorrow, I'll sell it to him. With this I'll pay off
my debt, then Fredo will make himself scarce, don't
worry. You won't have to come and cook my soup or
water down my booze while I'm over there.

Now it's evening and the hunters are preparing
for tomorrow's outing. In Valhalla they don't talk
about anything else: the wolf is bleeding, they say.
He's holed up, injured, trapped; the dogs will smell

him, and the first one to find him will take home the fur. They drink and psyche each other up.

Johnny says to me: Yo, Eighteen Hundred, have you ever tried gin and prosecco?

Not yet, I say.

It's like whisky and beer, but mixed together.

Let's try.

Did I mention why they call him Johnny? It's because he once walked around in cowboy boots and hat. Now he's hung up his hat but he's still Johnny: around here, when they give you a name you can never shake it off. He asks the bartender for two glasses of prosecco and a small glass of gin on the side.

Gordon's or Tanqueray? the bartender says.

Go for the Tanqueray, Johnny says.

When they're in front of him, he pours a tear of gin into one glass and a long shot into the other. He thinks I didn't see.

Did you just give me more? I say.

You're the one celebrating, he says.

I drink it and it seems decent to me. The only problem is that the gin warmed the prosecco. They should keep it in the fridge.

What kind of work do you do now, Johnny?

Night watchman at the dam.

Backbreaking work, eh?

I listen to the radio a lot. How was the cocktail?

Good.

Another round?

Gladly.

Now even a blind man can see the move: he pretends to pour himself the gin, but gives it all to me. He nudges the guy next to him. This is another little game from the old days: get the dumbest guy in the company hammered, and then see how straight he walks.

Welcome home, Eighteen Hundred, Johnny says, raising a glass.

When I hear that word, something in me breaks its banks and overflows. I down the drink, take the hatchet I have in my belt, lift it high and bring it down on his forehead. *Salut*. The iron and bone make the noise of rocks clonking underwater when the river's in full spate. The bartender hollers. Johnny goes down and only then does the blood start to gush.

*

Now that I'm saying goodbye to this valley, my brother chasing me with his flashing light on, I feel like I'm passing by all the bars of my life. I go downstairs and greet them one by one, like when it was late at night and we ended up at the service station for breakfast. Goodbye Sporting, goodbye Fior di Roccia, farewell Golosone, godspeed Valhalla. A white, a Braulio, a Baileys, a double malt red! Don't stop me, Brother: think of your wife, think of your daughter. Goodbye Sole e Neve, a beer! goodbye La Ruota, a whisky! goodbye Silly Monkey, hands off, I got this round. Don't stop me, Brother, don't stop me: think about what you have that I don't. Goodbye Laghetto, goodbye Woodland, goodbye Bar Alpino, goodbye. Look at this black river, look how clear everything is.

Woman in the Water

In the summer of 1979, a younger Elisabetta is in a bathing suit, on a smooth, warm rock, where the river widens into a transparent pool. She is seventeen and comes to Valsesia in August, after the sea. The river is full of water: if you entered the rapids, they would take you away. That spot, however, is a natural swimming pool; holidaymakers come to swim there. The boy who is with her, though, has never been there. Elisabetta watches him, amused. He's naked except for his white underwear, so uncomfortable even though this is his river, his valley.

You should take them off, she says to him, laughing. No one'll see us.

Here there's always someone who's watching, he says.

Luigi – that's his name – stretches out a foot

and tests the temperature of the water. Elisabetta, covered in freckles from the sun she got on the beach, looks at his pale back, the definition of his muscles, the line where his skin suddenly darkens on his neck and arms. She wouldn't admit to herself that the attraction she feels for him is anthropological, or political, if you will. In Milan she's in the student collective of the Liceo Manzoni, here in Valsesia she's only ever had flings with other holidaymakers. Summer romances. This boy, on the other hand, is twenty-one years old and dropped out in the eighth grade. It's not just a summer fling.

She says: Why do you call the Sesia her?

That's what we call her, he says, with his hands clinging to a rock. You're the only ones who call her it.

Interesting, she says. A female river.

She's about to make a comment about the maternal nature of water, but bites her tongue as she remembers what he told her about losing his mother as a child. She thinks of Thetis, the Greek goddess of rivers and springs. Achilles' mother who makes him invulnerable by immersing him in the Styx, except for his heel. She decides to let it go: she doesn't want to play schoolmarm to the noble savage – that's not what she's here for. What fascinates her is the real life in him.

She stands up on the boulder. She feels the warm rock under her toes.

So, she says, if I strip, will you strip too?

Don't do it, he says.

Yes or no?

They'll see you. There must be an old guy with binoculars somewhere.

Elisabetta does it. She's not interested in any old men with binoculars, but in that boy there. She takes off her bathing suit, throws it on the rock, takes a step and dives into the Sesia – her, as she'll refer to the river from now on.

*

In the fifteen years she's been with Luigi, she's learned many such things. Another is that the valley has one side in the sun and one side in the shade. On the sunny side there are fields, on the shaded side, woods. In the shade, the trees turn yellow earlier in the fall, and the snow stays longer in the spring, when an early green in the sun already offers hope that winter is over. There are animals of the sun and those of the shade: domestic on one side, wild on the other. But the streams that descend from both sides all flow into the same river, where you can no longer distinguish or separate them.

She taught him things, too. For example, how a woman wants to be caressed. Luigi rushed in the beginning, he did everything quickly and in silence.

So who did you do it with before? she asked him once.

Better I don't tell you, he answered.

But then he applied himself with great dedication; his hands learned to touch her. That's one thing that Elisabetta immediately liked about Luigi: his was a type of intelligence that had disappeared in the city: with his hands he could learn anything, probably even how to play the piano, if he put his mind to it. She loved watching him work wood. Wood was his element, his side in the sun.

The shadow side, though, as she soon discovered, had to do with alcohol. Alcohol had to do with his father and brother. Elisabetta had never seen anyone drink the way they did: they could stay drunk for several days at a time, going to bed drinking and waking up drinking. And meanwhile working, driving, hunting, making love, without anyone who didn't know them noticing anything. But if you knew them, you could tell they were drunk by certain details. Luigi no longer felt the cold, for example, or pretended to remember the conversations from the night before. In reality, he had memory lapses that lasted entire days. Who knows where he went when the alcohol kidnapped him and took him away. It was as if drinking reconnected him to that wild side in the woods, a wintry part of himself, which Elisabetta connected to his mother, whom he had lost. He had never been violent, except with words. She learned from drunken words not to get hurt. When he came back, he was sweeter than usual, even more needy of her.

That day at the river, she didn't expect to fall in love like that. She came to stay at twenty-one, when she could no longer bear the distance between them. They went to live in a two-room flat down in the valley. Coming from Fontana Fredda, it was the first time he had a real bathroom. It seemed incredible but he had grown up in a house where you did it in a hole in the floor, and it went straight down to the stable. Against the advice of her parents, she left Milan and her university and began to support herself in Valsesia with seasonal jobs, the country-side in summer, restaurants in winter, while Luigi worked in carpentry with the plan of opening a shop of his own. That was real life, after reading so much about it in her books.

When they had been living together for a year, he was the one who asked her to get married, unexpectedly. Elisabetta had never thought about marriage. She got there by continuing not to think about it and she found herself as a wife one morning in May, on the lawn in front of a small church dedicated to San Lorenzo. Neither his father nor her parents were there. After lunch, they said goodbye to their few friends and went alone to swim in the river.

*

It's November 1994 and Elisabetta leaves the restaurant where she now works. It's already dark, there's been a little rain. She gets in the car; she knows she smells like fried food, and she wonders whether to go home and take a shower, or let it go and do what she has to do. She remembers how she used to smile at the shepherds who smelled of stables and perfume, because they put it on without having washed properly, and she thinks: everyone stinks of the life they lead, they should just be proud of it. What's the difference between goat and fryer? She turns unsteadily into the back road; driving in the dark on slick roads makes her uneasy. She drives for a couple of kilometres, stops at the side of the road, leaves the keys in the ignition as she gets out of the car, and enters the grocery store.

Ciao, Franca, she says. She would like some fresh vegetables but in the boxes there are only onions, potatoes, a wilted lettuce, a few soft carrots. Low season.

You don't have any fruit?

The truck should be coming, Franca says behind the counter.

All good here?

Yeah, pretty much.

How's your mum doing?

From behind the woman comes the sound of the television. There's a door ajar that opens into a living room, and Elisabetta catches a glimpse of Franca's husband on the sofa. House and shop. When the entrance bell rings, like now that she's entered, one of the two simply gets up and comes over to serve. It's always worked that way. She remembers when she came on holiday and Franca's mother ran the shop, which hasn't changed otherwise.

After shopping, she stops at the public library. There is only the librarian at the loan desk, a girl who recently arrived. She also got married here, and Elisabetta feels like she's seeing herself again at the beginning. Antonella, her name is. She was happy with this job, then she discovered that practically no one uses the library, apart from middle-school students and this kind woman.

Elisabetta has a book to return. Robert Graves, *The White Goddess*. The librarian heats up some water with the electric kettle. They sit down to drink tea.

I have another person for the reading group, says Elisabetta. So now there's five of us.

Who is it? Antonella asks.

A lady who comes to the trattoria.

Have you thought about what to read?

You're the librarian.

Antonella thinks about it. She watches Betta, cup in hand. The fried odour must have reached her by now.

So what did you study? she asks.

I went to classical high school. Two years of literature at university, then I stopped and came here.

You're not sorry?

For what, quitting school?

That too.

No, not at all. I wouldn't go back.

A half-truth. The fact is that Elisabetta knows there's no going back. The river flows one way only. She has never wasted time with regrets, it's a blessing in her character.

She says: This coming winter is your second, isn't it?

It is.

The second is the hardest. Be patient.

Why is it the hardest?

Because the first is new. It's a discovery.

And by the third you get used to it?

Let's think about a good book.

*

Ultimately, the women of the valley kept each other company by having children. She didn't immediately feel the need. She was young and there were many things she liked about that life: the woods and the river, above all. The summer full of water and the winters with lots of snow, the agricultural cycle, learning from the farmers. And her books, which never left her alone. Elisabetta is a woman who has been kept company, since she was a girl, as much by writers as by real people: she talks to them, they talk to her.

There were some who helped her live here. Chekhov: he could have been the valley's chief doctor. Flannery O'Connor, that strange girl who lives with her mother. And Karen Blixen, the lady all alone in the old family villa. Here was a woman who did not complain about her fate: abandoned by her husband, afflicted by syphilis, with the burden of a farm always on the verge of failure, yet her gaze was full of wonder, her voice full of grace. She sang about the love between a noblewoman and a wild, indomitable being, which she called Africa, which could easily have been called Valsesia. She had spent eighteen years there, then she returned to Denmark and started writing to cure her nostalgia: Elisabetta understood her.

Once married, Luigi opened the carpentry shop. It didn't last long, because he was good with wood but terrible with accounts, and she was the least suitable person to help him. After the failure he took part in a competition and with the help of an acquaintance was taken into the Forestry Department. Late, to make a career. Being an entry-level agent at thirty meant being ten years behind those who had joined after the military. He did it for the pay cheque, for the two of them, for the structure he was trying to impose on his life. At first, taking orders made him nervous – the uniform seemed to make him itch – but he almost always worked outdoors, and he liked that. He came back home in excellent spirits from days spent counting partridges and black grouse, or following the reintroduction of deer. At dinner he told her about it: Imagine, Betta, a couple captured in Yugoslavia, put to sleep with tranquilisers and transported to Valsesia, where they were freed in the woods. Who knows if those deer noticed that they had travelled a thousand kilometres in their sleep. The female was probably pregnant. The male had just lost his antlers. The first deer rack scattered in Valsesia for who knows how many years: he would have liked to find it and bring it home. Now he no longer talked about carpentry. Chapter closed. She thought of the boy in the river, about whom she had understood almost nothing at the time, of the distant places from which the two of them came, of the long journey they were making together.

*

It's a year before Alfredo's return, October 1993. I'm going to visit Chief Kinanjui, Elisabetta says to herself in the morning. Like Karen Blixen, who once a week visits the Kikuyu chief in his hut. She takes the car and leaves the town: after the library, the middle school, the town auditorium, she passes a bridge and the road becomes narrower and poorly asphalted. Her hands get a little sweaty, there aren't even guardrails on the hairpin turns. As you go up, you begin to come across small vegetable gardens, some piles of wood, a mule. The houses have stone walls. Rocks emerging from the ground, undammed torrents, civilisation fading away. After the last bend, the panorama changes decidedly, the southern exposure always comes unexpectedly, and Elisabetta finds herself on this plateau overlooking the valley as if from a terrace. Fontana Fredda. The road ends there, with a village of dilapidated houses, and then only woods and pastures. The Kikuyu village.

She walks the last stretch to the old man's house.

She says: Ciao, Grato.

He doesn't answer her. He's not that old after all, it's the alcohol that's aged him before his time. He's focused on a job: with trembling hands, he's trying to sharpen the chainsaw.

She pretends that he said: Ciao, Elisabetta.

I brought you eggs. Is the stove turned on?

A nod of the chin. It means yes.

So I'll go make you some coffee, okay?

Elisabetta leaves him alone. The chainsaw is secured with a clamp to a wooden bench on the lawn in front of the house. All the work is done there, summer and winter, unless it's really pouring. When she returns with the cup, she watches him: what Grato needs to do is pass the file over each tooth of the chainsaw. Luigi showed her once. Two or three passes, important that it's always the same number, with a quick movement and slight rotation. As if it were a screw coming in, see? But the father's hands are not those of his son, not any more, and precision work has become so frustrating for him. He swears at the tool.

Elisabetta sits on the bench and hands Grato his breakfast. In the cup, she beat the egg yolk with the sugar, and then she poured the coffee. Like with children, she manages to feed him with some tricks. Eggs are now a fundamental ingredient of his diet, otherwise he no longer eats anything.

Grato sits next to her. He takes the cup, smells it, there's no alcohol inside. He makes a disappointed face. But he takes a sip, and he likes what he tastes.

Good, he says, in a faint voice.

Elisabetta looks out over the valley from the bench. There's snow already up above, a mist below. This sky, this light. She just can't understand why everyone left.

Grato, she says, have you heard about the chairlift?

Yeah, I heard.

It'll bring something new, eh? Some folks will even come back up here to live. Might be nice.

Might.

You don't think so?

The old man raises a hand and points to the road where it disappears behind the village. His finger is gnarled, arthritic. It's Chief Kinanjui talking, saying: Once, from that bend over there, the first chainsaw came. It was so big that they carried it up on a mule, took two fellas to handle it. We put the two-man saw away. So now to cut plants you need fuel.

It's easier though, isn't it?

Grato pretends not to hear. He coughs. He says: Then came the asphalt road, before that you could only go up the mule track.

When was that?

Not long ago. Twenty years.

The road came, and then?

People went down to work in the factory. Everyone disappeared. Now it's time for the chairlift.

We'll see. It's just a project.

A goddamned one.

Grato finishes drinking his coffee. He has some egg foam in his moustache, but the tremor has diminished. It's the sugar, Elisabetta thinks. She knows that he is right about the harm of progress, but she also knows that Chief Kinanjui is destined for extinction. She looks at his profile and finds Luigi's there. The same straight, ancient nose. She happens to look at the father and imagine how his son will become when he grows up.

Then Grato's eyes freeze on one point. She notices that he's seen something. She follows his gaze and discovers a large bird perched at the top of a larch. An eagle. There's no mistaking. Luigi explained to her that there's a couple in the upper valley, and one day from the car he showed her one circling. He told her that eagles stay together for life. They mainly hunt marmots, but also chamois kids, and sometimes chickens. They cover a radius of ten kilometres around the nest and don't let any adversaries within range. The eaglet, once grown, has to go elsewhere, and this could be a young male looking for a home.

Bring me the rifle, says Grato, staring at that bird so as not to lose sight of it. He seems in a trance.

What?

It's in the cellar. It's already loaded. Quick.

No, Grato.

Move it!

Elisabetta doesn't move. Luigi told him: his father shoots at anything that breathes. The poacher's nature is so ingrained in him that he can't see a wild animal without the desire to shoot it. One day or another he'll have to go up and arrest him, or at least take away his rifle.

If he had really taken it away from him, who knows. Maybe Grato would have found another way of killing himself. She never talked about it with Luigi. For Elisabetta, those are the gears of destiny: it's the last time she sees the old man alive.

The eagle takes flight from the top of the larch, and she notices how it doesn't take off by flapping its wings, like other birds. It spreads them wide and leaps into the updraft rising from the valley floor. How beautiful it must be, she thinks, to leap into the wind like that. Grato mutters a word. An ugly word, from a snarling old man, for his son's outsider wife. This time she's the one pretending not to hear.

*

In the bathroom, she looks at herself in the mirror. She is thirty-two years old and looks a little neglected. When she returns to her parents in Milan, she now immediately notices the girls on the street, their hair and clothes. The styles have changed a lot since she left. She turns and looks at her belly in profile: the bump is starting to show. Soon everyone in the valley will know. And maybe at that point, yes, she'll be one of the valley people too. A few months had passed since Grato's death when one evening she asked Luigi: What do you think if we have a child? This time it was her idea. She didn't bother wasting time thinking about the relationship between the two facts, the loss of a father and the desire for a child, even though she knew it had to be there. Luigi answered: I've been hoping you'd say that for a while.

After the shower, she has dinner alone, with the radio on. On the cultural channel, a woman's voice fades into a piano piece. Elisabetta listens to music, eats rice salad and looks out the window. The petrol pump sign shines over the dark street. She thinks of the men in their homes who are cleaning their rifles at this hour. She heard them talking about it at work, even though people are cautious around her, she's the wife of a forestry cop. But some news can't stay secret: at dawn a group of hunters will gather at the Roman bridge, and from there they'll go up the Sesia in formation. Others will stand further up, at pre-established points, waiting for that dog, or wolf, to come within range. She wonders what will become of the female, the little white dog she saw this morning.

The phone rings, Elisabetta gets up and goes to answer it. Sometimes she lets it ring. But this evening she'd like some company.

Ciao, Mamma, she says.

Have you heard about that book? her mother's voice asks.

What book?

You don't have the radio on?

I was lost in thought.

The one about Dolcino and Margherita.

They listen to the same channel and her mother calls her to comment on the broadcast, as if they were in the same kitchen.

She says: You know, the heretics.

Apostolics, Elisabetta corrects her.

Weren't they hiding there in Valsesia?

Yes, in Rassa. Heretics for someone else.

Well, they said that Margherita was a wealthy girl; she came from a noble family from Trent. Until Dolcino passed through to preach his doctrine, and she fell in love.

With him or his doctrine?

They wound up getting together. You tell me.

Her mother must have been really happy.

Margherita wasn't very happy either.

And how do you know?

Because after four years Margherita was tied to a stake. They burned her alive before his eyes.

Only four years?

Elisabetta takes the phone to the window and sits there again. She can hear the music on the other end of the line. She thinks of the house where she grew up: the living room, the armchairs, the carpet, the paintings on the walls with Alpine views. Outside, the tanker has arrived that supplies the petrol station twice a week. In her parents' paintings, though, there are peasant women in the fields, little white churches blushing in the sunset.

Don't worry, she says. No one here will burn me alive.

Is Luigi home? her mother asks.

No. He's out.

On shift tonight?

Yes, Mamma.

With a pregnant wife, couldn't he arrange to stay home in the evenings? Didn't you tell me his commander is a woman?

And what should a woman commander do?

She should know that another woman, a pregnant one, is home alone. It's called female solidarity.

And she's called *chief inspector*.

Her mother scoffs into the phone. An ambulance passes on the road. Flashing lights on, siren fading into the distance. Maybe her mother is also looking outside: the tenement courtyard, the roof tiles on the opposite side, the railed walkway balconies. The November sky of Milan, when the fog reflects the lights of the city.

Listen, her mother says. If you don't want to come here, I might just go up there in a little while. At least towards the end of the pregnancy.

There's loads of time before the end.

You think. April.

C'mon, Mamma.

She says goodbye abruptly. She'll call back in ten minutes, anyway. When she hangs up, Elisabetta thinks: April. It's crazy to think about April now. There's the whole winter in between, and winter needs to be faced without looking too far ahead. She imagines making her mother's bed on the couch: Luigi coming back with his uniform full of mud and finding her there in her nightgown.

What her mother doesn't know, and what she is careful not to tell her, is that every now and then he sleeps outside. On the river, maybe. Or at his father's house. Or he takes a sleeping bag to certain places in the valley that only he knows. It happens after they've argued, and if they've argued, alcohol is almost always involved. Once she asked him what he does during those nights: he lights a fire, drinks a bottle. She never doubted it was true. Over the years, she's got used to these lonely nights as a part of her marriage. She has a husband who sometimes sleeps with her, and sometimes in the woods. Elisabetta will get tired of it, one day not too far off.

So tonight she didn't expect him to come back. She wakes up hearing him come into the room, dropping his clothes to the floor. She feels her covers lift and soon after his hand on her hip, where he likes to hold her when they're in bed together. She's turned the other way. His hand is still cold from outside.

What time is it? she asks.

Late, Luigi says.

Your brother?

He's gone.

She turns to him and smells the whisky on his breath. Whisky, cigarettes, and another smell that must have stayed in his beard and hair. The smell of damp earth, of rain, of the riverbank. In the darkness she searches for him with her hand, finds a shoulder, his neck, caresses it.

What, he left?

He cracked open a guy's head, at the bar. With a hatchet. Then took off.

He cracked his head open? He killed him?

No, the guy's in intensive care. Closer to that edge than this one, but alive for now.

You went to the hospital?

Yeah. I even know him.

Who is it?

Just some poor asshole.

And where's your brother?

I don't know where. In Canada.

Luigi sobs. Elisabetta can feel, with her fingers, that his cheek is wet. Is this the kind of real life she wanted? Now she knows the lament of a drunk crying in the night. She knows what a man's head blown up by a gunshot looks like. She's seen a lot of reality, no doubt. Luigi cries in the dark; he can't hold back any more. Through alcohol's fault or merit, it all comes out at once: he cries for his brother, he cries for his father, he cries for himself.

We'll make the house no matter what, he says. Don't worry.

My love, she says. My love.

She kisses him on the cheek, on the eyes. She kisses his lips that taste like whisky, his beard that tastes like river.

*

In the morning she lets him sleep, puts a towel in a bag and leaves the house. She crosses the road, the petrol pump, the woods beyond, and takes a path that goes down. A few kilometres further up the valley, the hunting posse should be finished by now. The Sesia is shallow these days; the frost has dried up the streams that feed it, but Elisabetta knows a pool where there is always water. She balances over the boulders as she walks to reach it. She stops at the larger and flatter one and sits down.

The Sesia welcomes her. Today she is so shallow, parts emerge that are nearly always underwater. The smooth logs look like sculptures. The most beautiful are the roots of the trees, so sinuous and twisted. Birch trees invite new beginnings. The voice of the river is barely a whisper: a pool, a rapid, a pool, then the bend where it changes direction. Like life turning.

Elisabetta undresses. It's cold, and she has discovered that it is important to breathe deeply. Her breathing warms her. She enters the water with one foot and then with the other. Even though she is used to it, there is always a moment when instincts revolt, and an effort of will is required. The water reaches her thighs, then her groin, then her ribs. She stops there. She places a hand on her belly and pronounces her invocation from within: Daughter, this is Sesia. Sesia, protect my little girl.

She stays there for a few seconds, then comes out of the water and dries off. She rubs hard to warm up and puts her clothes on: socks, jeans, wool sweater, boots. Her skin is covered by a nice tingling sensation, the capillaries that had contracted reopen, her blood flows.

She has just put the towel back in the bag when she sees movement in the shrubs. A dog? Yes, it's yesterday's dog. The white one, she's watching her. Elisabetta looks around and realises that the male is no longer there. The female is alone on the river, watching her fearfully but needily, without deciding to approach or flee. She should be terrified of men at this point, but she can't live without them. Maybe she senses this is a woman. She's tempted to trust her.

Fifteen years earlier, Elisabetta lies naked, in the

sun, on that hot and smooth boulder, and waits for the boy to arrive.

Fifteen years later, she kneels down and reaches out to the dog.

Come, she says. Come here.

Oh, My Father's House

Last night I dreamed I was running through the woods. It was evening, just before dark, and the hunting dogs were chasing me. I could hear them behind me, I could hear the noise dogs make when hunting down game, the tree branches scratching me, tearing my clothes. I don't know if I was the man I am now or the child of the past, but that wasn't the forest where I grew up, where the light passes through the fir and larch trees. It was a denser and wilder forest, one of those forests at the bottom of the valley, the evening air blowing and the plants stirring, birch, rowan, ash, alder, willow, hawthorn. I couldn't see those dogs from hell; I only had their barking in my ears. I ran and ran and my heart was hammering.

Then I saw an ivy door, as I call it when two trees are enveloped by ivy passing from the branches of one to the other, and I dived through it. On the other side was my father's house. His actual house. Not the dark and sad house of now, but a big, beautiful house, with windows lit like headlights. Truth be told, those windows were shining. As I got closer, I realised what all that light was. I thought: He really did it, Fredo really set it on fire, my father's house is in flames, and I woke up. Outside the dream, the phone was ringing.

*

Elisabetta had left. It took me a moment to understand it, and I got up to answer. I already imagined the Carabinieri, the police, someone calling me from headquarters; I had completely forgotten about the notary. The secretary said they were waiting for us in the office. There in the kitchen, with a pasty voice, I had to apologise and explain to her that we weren't going ahead with it. She must have thought: this guy was supposed to come here to buy a house and stayed in bed sleeping. She was annoyed, but I understood that it wasn't such a rare occurrence. An inconvenience of the trade. After all, if there are people who don't show up for the priest . . .

I hung up and realised I was naked. How come I'm naked? I thought. I remembered that last night, or whenever, Betta and I had made love. In the kitchen she had left me a slice of pie on a saucer and the moka pot ready – I just had to turn on the stove. Under the saucer there was a note that I looked at as the coffee rose up: she had drawn two trees on it, a larch and a birch, with a small heart in the middle. One of the narrow, skinny hearts she draws. I don't deserve a woman like that, I thought. I looked at the kitchen with all of her things, the coloured cups, the calendar of flowers, the things of hers that soften my life. I poured the coffee and ate the pie, a blueberry pie. I think they were the blueberries we'd picked in August and I remembered her with her blue fingers and blue mouth.

Then I called the hospital to find out if that guy was alive or dead.

Alive, that's all I found out. But he still hadn't regained consciousness.

*

That morning I was free, but I didn't want to hear what people were saying, so I went back to yesterday's place, the Rottweiler place. On the riverbank, the scant snow was all crushed. Hunters' footprints – not many – I counted four different soles and maybe as many dogs. I started following them. It might take a while, but I had time and didn't mind walking. I had to work off two days of drinking.

As I expected, the Sesia hollowed out into the hill further up. Not exactly a gorge, but the banks got steep and it was a hassle to go halfway up the slope. The simplest route was the riverbed. I stopped trying to jump from one stone to another. There was no avoiding getting wet, so I put my feet in and didn't pay any mind. Nothing like ice water to chase the alcohol out of your body. It's like the devil running away from a prayer. Everything in the woods was so quiet that I began to calm down too: I went upriver, listened to the current, I discovered certain holes that, with just a little more water, would have been amazing pools. We should really go back, I thought. It would be good for Betta and me. At one point, a little trout even jumped between my feet.

I found the dog after an hour of walking. They'd left him there, the Valsesia killer, stuck between two boulders. Or maybe they'd killed him higher up and the current had carried him down for a while until the rocks stopped him. The body was half-submerged – brilliant idea to leave a carcass to rot in the river – so I took it by the legs, pulled it out of the water, laid it on the bank. Soaked as it was, it looked like nothing but bones.

I saw right away that it was no wolf. You lost the bet, Fredo. It had a wolf's head, and the grey fur might have been a wolf's, but then black patches appeared on the hind quarters, like a dog. Go figure the cross between what and what. He had a gash on his side, probably a reminder from the Rottweiler, and a bullet hole above his shoulder. At least they took him out on the first try. His muzzle was all marked with scars, which didn't look like bites from any dogs, wolves, tigers or lions. Those were the canings he'd taken during his life.

I wondered for a moment, thought about how to take him away, whether to go back and look for a backpack or build a kind of litter with branches. Then I gave up on anything creative. It was just one of those jobs you have to face, like the slope that was waiting for me. I put him on my shoulder. He weighed about thirty kilos. I grasped the front paws in my right hand and the hind ones in my left. Then I went up along the riverbank and straight ahead.

The undergrowth was all rotten leaves and hidden roots. I trudged along with the weight on my shoulders and the water dripping down my back. I adjusted him every two steps. Careful not to slip. Meanwhile, I said to myself: Look at what a great job you got for yourself; you've been picking up dead dogs for days. The dog gravedigger. His head, that poor head, was lolling to one side and banging against me.

It really wasn't much of a hike. It's small, my valley. One hundred metres of uphill and I found myself on the back road. I put the dog down, hid it in the bushes, and walked towards my Suzuki. Not along the river, but on the road. Some cars slowed down as they passed me. I was soaking wet, but I'd got so hot going up that hill that my shoulders were steaming.

*

I drove, went up the valley. With the dead dog in the trunk, I slowly passed the hardware store, the grocery store, the tobacco shop, so that whoever was supposed to see me among the villagers would see me. Without having decided beforehand, at the crossroads for Fontana Fredda I turned and went up. It was as if my father's house was calling me.

For eight kilometres, I thought about what my father was like when I was a kid. Not a bad father, just a miserable hard-luck case. I remembered when he took us to see the villas around Valsesia. He told us about people who had made money with textiles, with cement. One had started by buying wool from shepherds, another by taking worthless land along the river. There was a loan shark who lent cash to farmers in exchange for a mortgage on their fields, tiny plots most of the time, little family fields. With that system the shark wound up owning half of Valsesia: then, to save his soul, he had a small church built dedicated to San Gratus, protector of crops from bad weather and of Christians from lightning. These villas that we went to see were almost always closed, except for certain spring Sundays when we sat in the car watching the rich people having lunch on their verandas. I don't know what sort of gusto my father got from that; all it did was make his blood bitter.

I made it up there and was convinced inside

myself that I would find a pile of smoking rubble. Instead, the house was still there; Fredo had only knocked down a plant in the garden. His, not mine. The larch was upright, and the fir was stretched out. I appreciated my brother's humour, even though I felt sorry for having lost what was an adult plant by now, but then I thought, at his expense, that the larch would grow better without the fir's shade. I unloaded the dog, wet as a rag, on the lawn and went to the stable to look for a shovel and pickaxe.

When I went out with the tools, Gemma was there, she was staring at the dog. Gemma is one of the last people still in Fontana Fredda – strange to say. She and my father hadn't spoken for years. With me and Betta, though, she had no problems, and she was happy when she found out that we'd be coming to live up here.

Luigi, she said. Ciao.

Ciao, Gemma.

What are you doing?

I'm burying this dog.

Was that your dog?

No. But I'm doing it anyway.

She thought about it. She said: Good boy.

I looked around and asked: What do you think, Gemma? Where should I put him?

Isn't it better to put him in the woods?

No, no. I want to keep him here in the yard.

I chose the corner on the side of the trees, near the larch and the fir stump. The wood was still white in the stump and you could count the notches from the axe blows. Fredo is good, I thought: I haven't seen a tree chopped down by hand in years. I took the pickaxe, raised it above my head and started going at it too.

It must have taken me half an hour to dig that hole. I pulled out many rocks. Everything under Fontana Fredda is stone, rocks with earth on top. I went down far enough so that any fox catching the scent wouldn't start scratching. I took the dog by the legs, dragged him into the hole, gave him a stroke on the snout, covered him with the bigger rocks and then with the smaller ones. Finally, what little earth there was. I was all sweaty when I sat down to admire my work. I lit a cigarette and looked at the standing larch, the lying fir and the dog's grave between the two of them.

Gemma was still there; she didn't miss a move.

Luigi, she said, is it true they're making a ski slope?

Yeah, it's true, I said.

When do they start?

April or May.

Are they gonna cut a lot of plants?

Well, I said, between the slope and the chairlift there's ten hectares of woods. At five hundred plants per hectare, that makes around five thousand. We have to go up and hammer them these days.

Hammer them?

Mark them with paint. Then in spring they'll come to cut them down.

Five thousand plants they're cutting?

I looked at her. The expression was more sad than doubtful. Very blue and disconsolate eyes.

What are you gonna do? I said. You can't ski in the middle of the woods.

What a shame, she said.

Gemma was right, of course. But since the dawn of time, men have been cutting down plants, mating beasts and bashing each other's heads in. If there's evil on this earth it is only of our own doing. I finished the cigarette, crushed it in the grass and thought about going down and getting the chainsaw to cut that fir into firewood, though it doesn't burn well in the stove, but I couldn't stand looking at it in my yard any more.

*

Later, I was driving up that road that I've driven a million times in my life, always the same, the dear old country road of my soul, when at a bend the valley turned and I found myself facing the Rosa glacier. She was shining so bright that it hurt my eyes. I don't know why, but I felt the need to pull over. I stopped the car on the side of the road and stared at that dazzling white against the sky. I often forget that at the top of this valley there's that mountain, that the river springs from there: down below us the shadow had already fallen long ago, while up there the glacier reflected the sun. It was like my father's house in the dream, tall, beautiful, bright. The salvation I was running towards. I looked at it through the windscreen and my father's house shone over this dark valley, where our sins lie, unatoned.

The Battle of the Trees

I was many forms before;
I was a torrent on the slope,
I was a salmon in the ocean,
I was the fog that wets your hair.

I was a girl, a dog,
a glass in the hands of the drinker,
the breath inside the harmonica,
the snow reflecting the moon.

From my high home,
where the icy water once rose,
I saw trees and green creatures
summoned to battle.

Willow in the vanguard
parried the assault.
Rowan behind
watched his back.

Dog Rose posed
resolute resistance,
armed with spearheads
that hurt the hands.

Oak's footfalls
the clamour of battle:
his name, stalwart
guardian in all tongues.

Holly and Hawthorn
pressed deftly.
Nettles furious
with Rhubarb as squire.

Fir, rough and wild,
Ash merciless:
no turning from attack
straight at the heart.

Birch, though offended,
did not arm like the others,
not out of cowardice
but of noble rank.

Blueberry and Gentian,
with no experience of war,
languished under cover
of the gallant Fern.

Heather offered solace
to the exhausted fighters,
resin-scented Pine
fell into their arms.

Worthy were Juniper,
with his bad fruit,
and unloved Scrub Pine
with his humble dress.

Bearberry with her dowry
stayed sullen at battle's edge,
slow-burning Elderberry
among the rising flames.

Rhododendron shrank
into compact ranks.
No step back for Raspberry
under enemy pressure.

Oaks, Sessile and Downy,
with Ivy covering them,
all fought, were felled,
and lay together.

Maple, despite his fury,
almost motionless:
fought through thick battle
with lofty lament.

Chestnut, before being
crushed with his sweet fruits,
caused great commotion,
gaining fame for bravery.

Beech struck with ardour.
Hornbeam stripped in the fray.
Plundering Fireweed
scattered by wind.

Larch raised the cry to him:
heaven and earth shook.
Branches with fresh shoots
stuck to the ground.

Stone Pine was last to fall.
His attack struck terror.
Pushed back, he then pushed,
levelling with fierce blows.

Now the trickling is silenced,
the stone rounded,
the great seas advance quickly
since I heard the battle cry.

And blessed Golden Rain
laughs forgotten
under the strangely
overhanging rock.

Birch top sprouts
from the stump:
in his patient vigour
people hope.

Wayfarers amazed,
wise men dismayed
by fresh clashes
like those just quelled.

Under the waning moon
a terrible fight,
and another about to rage
fully under the sun.

Yet I, though unnoticed,
as then I was not in this form,
fought, O trees, among your ranks
on Fontana Fredda's field.

Author's Note

I grew up in a house where there wasn't much music but, luckily, I had an older sister with a stereo and some cassettes. One of these was Bruce Springsteen's *Nebraska*. I remember the cover perfectly, with the musician's name and the title in red on a black background, and the black-and-white photo of a plain seen from behind a windscreen. The slightly slanted horizon, the sky thick with clouds, a reflection on the hood of the car, the road running straight through bare fields. At the beginning of the nineties, I fell in love with this album without really knowing why, since I didn't understand the lyrics. The music is as stripped as it gets: three chords (I discovered this much later, when trying to play it), guitar, harmonica and Springsteen's indistinct murmuring, singing with his mouth closed, or to himself, like you would at night in a dark room. Or maybe in that car cruising through Nebraska. I listened to it again and again, rewinding the tape: those cassettes got ruined over time, but it was okay because it added a dirtier edge to the sound, as if from some distant radio station caught by the car. I haven't stopped listening to it, and thirty years have passed. I really think it's the album I've listened to the most in my life.

*

I had to take a long journey through American literature before returning to *Nebraska* and understanding it better (here, I thank Leonardo Colombati and his precious study of the work). Meanwhile, the genesis: in the autumn of 1981 Springsteen was thirty-two years old and had just returned from his *The River* tour. That album had established him as a global rock star. He performed 140 concerts in a year, sold out both in America and Europe. There was no woman in his life, but he did have an adoptive family, the E Street Band, which dispersed when they got back to their base. Each on his own account for a while. But in fact, Bruce didn't have 'his own account', apart from a father with whom relationships were always difficult, who later became the most famous father of American rock (because of all his son's songs about him). The young man had also been evicted from his house, so he rented another one in his native New Jersey and went to live there. The idea was to write new songs, but he was alone, it was the beginning of winter, and the year he had just spent had taken its toll on him. The adrenaline and the crowds. Life on tour. A grim mood fell over him, one that Melville had described as 'a damp, drizzly November'.

In the evening, in that house, he began to watch mostly noir and violent films, such as Charles Laughton's *The Night of the Hunter* and Terrence Malick's *Badlands*. He read a lot. He would later say that this was the moment in his life when the inspiration for his songs stopped being other songs and became books. He would quote James M. Cain's *The Postman Always Rings Twice*, and especially Flannery O'Connor. Flannery O'Connor is a cornerstone for those, like me, who come from the short-story tradition. She was Catholic, of Irish origin (Springsteen is half Irish and half Italian, the most Catholic mix there is in America), lived in the South of the United States between the 1920s and

1960s, had a degenerative disease and died young after having spent a lot of time bedridden. Obviously, her stories were sombre. They were the true dark stories of the time. Thieves, murderers, one-legged girls, street preachers. A memorable one was called 'The River', and 'The River' was also the song from which Springsteen wanted to start again.

That tune had come out somewhat by chance a couple of years earlier. Until then, he had always written stuff like 'cut loose like a deuce . . . but till then, tramps like us, baby, we were born to run'. Then, unexpectedly, thinking about his sister's life, this beautiful song was born, about a couple. Him, raised in a valley where all they teach you is to 'do like your daddy done'. Her, seventeen when they met. She got pregnant right away. There's a shotgun wedding, a union card, work in a construction company. As kids, they often went swimming in the river, but over time they went there less and less. The river dries up, love dries with it. Recession comes and he loses his job. This isn't a story by Flannery O'Connor: it's a story by Raymond Carver, another author Springsteen read. Carver's debut book, *Will You Please Be Quiet, Please?* was published in 1976, and his second, *What We Talk*

About When We Talk About Love, in 1981, the same year as the song.

What music could go with stories like that? Who sang about the unemployed, the wretched, the petty thieves and the broke in American music? We need to go back to the folk music of the Great Depression, which Bob Dylan had already drawn on. The stories that Steinbeck told in literature with *The Grapes of Wrath* and *Of Mice and Men* were put into song by Pete Seeger, Hank Williams and Woody Guthrie. Voice, harmonica, and 'this machine kills fascists', as Guthrie had written on his guitar. Springsteen, the son of a worker from New Jersey, who grew up on a street with Italians on one side and Irish on the other, at thirty-two years old decides to take a break from rock 'n' roll, and use folk to try to tell those stories, which he also knows.

*

No one knows how moments of grace come to artists. It's a mystery. They can come from good times or from bad times. From quiet, from chaos, from pain, from a good marriage, or the end of a marriage – you just can't know. But without a doubt, one of those moments happened to Springsteen in the autumn of 1981. In the space of a few weeks, he wrote the ten songs of *Nebraska*, as well as others that would end up on subsequent albums. To record the demo, he asks his sound engineer to put together a small recording studio for him at home. The sound engineer sets him up with a four-track recorder, which means that for each song he'll be able to record three instruments plus the voice separately, and then mix them himself. So voice, guitar, harmonica and percussion, a simple tambourine. Other times, the fourth track is dedicated to the choruses, as he called them, even if listening to the record they seem more like howls.

What was it like to spend Christmas and New Year's Eve in that empty house? I remember a story by Carver, who said: 'The holidays are always the most difficult period.' (He was referring to alcohol.) Maybe at Christmas Bruce would have gone to his parents' place; for New Year's, he must have been invited to a party. Then on 3 January 1982, he turns on the recorder, sits down and starts playing. One song after another, he records them all. What a day.

In spring he gathers the band in the studio and after a good winter's rest he puts his musicians to work. They listen to the tape with the demos. They arrange them: add bass, drums, saxophone, keyboards and electric guitar. They do several takes, trying to build a nice sound. Then at one point they look at each other and everyone agrees, Springsteen included: those songs were better before. All the beauty was in the cassette that he had recorded himself, murmuring and howling. He doesn't even need to try to get it better. So what we hear today, when *Nebraska* comes out of our powerful (or just meagre) digital equipment, is Bruce Springsteen himself singing in his little room in New Jersey on 3 January 1982.

In the same months Raymond Carver was writing his best stories: *Cathedral* came out in 1983, shortly after *Nebraska*. Those stories and those songs are in dialogue with each other. Carver died in 1988, time enough to listen to the album and I think even love it, but I haven't been able to find out if the two ever met.

*

Taliesin was a sixth-century Welsh bard, a Bruce Springsteen of his time, if he really existed. The obscure poem 'Cad Goddeu', or 'The Battle of the Trees', is attributed to him, where memories of an ancient war, magic formulas and, according to scholars, an alphabet, called Beithe-luis-nuin from the first three letters that compose it, are hidden (birch, rowan, ash): each tree a letter, a lunar month, a mythical hero, a human character. I don't know if Mario Rigoni Stern had read it, but he often mentions the Celtic calendar in his *Arboreto salvatico*. I took the liberty of rewriting some lines of the poem, thinking about the trees in my woods and the things that are happening now.

*

Finally, Valsesia is a beautiful valley that descends from Monte Rosa, our mother mountain. I go there every now and then on foot from my house. I have also gone there by canoe because the Sesia is one of the most beautiful rivers to paddle down through the rapids, one of the last in the Alps not to have been levelled with berms, and for long stretches it's still wild. Valsesia has a solid tradition as a refuge for persecuted people and minorities – from Fra Dolcino to the Walser people to the partisans of the Resistance – and a working-class soul clearly visible in the valley below. For us, however, on our side of Monte Rosa, it's the place where the bad weather comes from. We even have a proverb that says: If the wind is from Valsesia, go home because it's going to rain. That valley is a funnel in which all the mists that rise from the plain between Novara and Vercelli end up, and it's bizarre to be standing on the watershed, or looking down from the Rosa glaciers, and regularly see clouds on one side and the sun on the other. It seems to be haunted by bad luck. The history of the valley is punctuated by floods, and due to its rainfall, it has earned the affectionate nickname of 'Italy's pissoir'. I've never been to the badlands of America, but Valsesia seemed like the right place to become my Nebraska.

Fountane, 2023
For Andrea, Davide and the Sottile refuge years. For Fede and our awakenings.
    With love.

About the Author

Paolo Cognetti was born in Milan and continues to divide his time between the city and his cabin in the Italian Alps. He is the author of *The Lovers* and *The Eight Mountains*, which was an international sensation: a bestseller in multiple languages and the winner of Italy's Premio Strega and France's Prix Médicis étranger. The film adaptation of *The Eight Mountains* won the 2022 Jury Prize at the Cannes Film Festival.

About the Translator

Stash Luczkiw is a US-born writer of poetry, fiction and journalism. He has translated various books from Italian and other languages into English.